MORE PR.

ISLA GRANDE

RICHARD HUGHES

Silver Mountain Press

Silver Mounatin Press
P.O. Box 12994
Tucson, Arizona 85732

Cover design: Ken Murray
Photograph: Gary Rumack

Library of Congress Cataloging-in-Publication Data

Hughes, Richard
    Isla Grande / Richard Hughes.
        p.   cm.
    ISBN 1-883721-10-5 (pbk.)
    1. Missing persons—Panama—Fiction.
    2. Americans—Panama—Fiction.
    I. Title.
    PS3558.U3877I85   1994
    813'.54—dc20   93-11422

Printed in the United States of America

For my father,
who was there

1

Whooshing the matted blinds back against the window screens and sucking the plastic lamp off its nightstand and onto the concrete floor, the front door of the room burst open. A shotgun blast shattered a hole in the wall above the headboard, spraying chunks of plaster over the pillows, dust snaking up through the glare of a half-dozen flashlight beams. A pack of men with rifles rushed into the room, the breech of a shotgun clicking.

One of the men lit a candle on the nightstand and flicked his gun muzzle toward the ceiling. The naked man and woman huddled on the bed sheets squirmed to the edge of the bed and stood up, the man grabbing a pair of underwear and khakis from the back of a chair while the woman stepped into a shift, fumbling the straps up over her shoulders and tugging at the zipper in back. The muzzle waved toward the door. The man and woman walked outside and onto the beach, where their heels squeaked in the sand.

A full moon hung in the sky above the island, moonlight silhouetting the pack of men, their sharp noses, their folded arms, their rifles pointed out in front of their chests. The couple stumbled ahead, clutching hands, kicking up glints of sand into the air with their toes.

On the slopes of the mountains, palm fronds rattled in the wind. Waves crashed on the shore. A troop of bats with their wings beating flew over the marchers and disappeared into the black at the other end of the beach. At the shoreline the man and woman stopped and turned around. The tide slapped at their feet. The woman raised her dress above her ankles and looked down. The man straightened his back and brushed the sweat from his lips, staring into the faces of the dark men who stood in a half-circle with their hair shining, their rifles aimed, their fingers creeping around the triggers. The shotguns exploded.

Pieces of flesh scattered into the air behind the two bodies. The couple crumpled on the sand. A wave rolled over them and back, leaving pools of saltwater in their stomachs and chests. Blood seeped into the sand. Another wave washed in and jerked the man's head toward the island and yanked it back again toward the sea.

The dark men herded around, prodding the holes with the tips of their rifles and lifting the woman's dress up above her waist. With a rope they wrapped the four red legs together and knotted the end of the line to the stern of a wooden canoe, dragging the corpses into the surf and clambering over the side of the boat, their shotguns clanging on the wood. They paddled the canoe toward the reef at the mouth of the cove, where the boat stuttered and lurched backward. The dark men stopped and turned around. Foam spewed over the two bodies in the water. A man in the back of the canoe stood up, grabbing the side with one hand and swearing at the noise. He leaned over and sliced the line with a machete and flopped back down into his seat.

An arm, severed at the elbow, thumped against the side of the hull. One of the men jabbed at it with his paddle, flipping over the long red fingernails, a knob of white bone glowing under the shreds of loose skin. A shark lunged forward and wrenched the limb between its teeth and dove. The men in the canoe cackled and turned away, digging their paddles into the water and pulling the canoe out the cove and into the gullies of the open sea.

2

Old men and boys and dead chickens jammed the back of the truck. Molded canvas hung over the top and down the sides. The passengers squatted on two wooden benches, the dead chickens swinging by the legs from the fists of the old men. The driver in the cabin sang along with a tune on the radio, working the steering wheel back and forth as the truck bounced over the mud holes in the road.

The old men and boys wore hats scrunched up on their foreheads with swatches of wavy black hair sticking out from under the rims and bushing over their ears. Beside their feet sacks of flour and rice covered the floor. The men stared at the knees of their starchy white pants, thistle fibers trapped in the weave.

A young man in jeans and a blue T-shirt sat at the end of one of the benches, an arm twined around the safety chain, the other clutching a duffel bag to his chest. He wiped the perspiration off his forehead and regripped the metal chain, swaying downhill with the rest of the passengers as the truck started to climb. Branches and vines scratched over the hood and across the canvas tarpaulin and down the back of the truck. They passed an old woman hiking up the mountain, her pleated dress sweeping through the dirt, the braided black tails of her hair leaping from side to side around her shoulders. She faded in the dust. At the top of the hill, they peaked and straightened out above clumps of bright green trees. Cliffs jutted down to the water, and all the way to the horizon stretched the sea.

The sky paled around the sun. The young man touched the canvas with his arm, and hot musty air seeped into the truck. The old men and boys slumped against each other and slept. The dead chickens jiggled across the benches as the road wound around the mountains above the coast, an island appearing and disappearing at the switches.

Seen full, the island lay alone a mile off shore, all green and lined with palm trees. Lime-colored mountains sloped up to a ridge twisting its length. Pink and yellow houses dotted the coast. A ring of white sand trimmed the shore, and the water in the channel turned turquoise and emerald and Prussian blue.

The young man reached forward, tapping an old man on the knee and pointing out the back of the truck at the island. The old peasant blinked open his eyes and turned, squinting into the sunlight and digging the end of his forefinger into his nose. He leaned his head back against the canvas.

"Isla Grande," he said, closing his eyes again and gluing snot on the edge of the wooden bench. Large blue flies crawled over the neck of his dead chicken.

The young man looked out the back as the island went out of view.

When the island was opposite the road and the road had descended to the coast, the truck stopped beside a pregnant woman in a yellow dress standing in front of a cluster of shacks. The woman tossed her hair away from her face with a hand and shifted a naked child higher on her hip. A girl grabbed at the woman's hem, got slapped in the mouth and grabbed again, spreading the fingers of her free hand across her nose and lips. The young man climbed out of the truck with his bag and paid the singing driver two American dollars. The driver nodded his head and put the money in a paper bag.

Running up from the shacks and gathering behind the pregnant woman and to her side came more children, chattering in high voices and slapping the dusty canvas on the truck as it sped away. Two of the taller boys scrambled for the duffel bag, wrestling it toward the shacks, followed by the young man and the children at his side shuffling through the clay, kicking at rocks.

A boy, darker than the others, tugged at the stranger's wrist and lifted it up to his ear, listening to the young man's watch as they walked. The bag disappeared behind a white shack with peeling walls, flakes of paint curled on the ground, music blaring through an opened window. Around the corner of the building drifted the sound of staggered clapping.

The stranger followed the two porters to the back of the house, where a wooden bench teetered against the wall. A group of children sat rocking their legs and giggling at an old man dancing in the dirt in front of the doorway. The old man watched his feet as he swanned in a circle, swiveling his hips, his arms branched in the air, his knees dipping up and down to the rhythm of an accordion. The dark boy tapped a finger on the watch.

The music stopped on a long chord, and the old man twirled around twice and grinned at the crowd. The children hooted and clapped and stomped their feet and whistled. The old man bowed and smoothed his white beard and his wrinkled white shirt. He walked over to the young man and clasped the stranger's hand and shook it.

"The music make me very happy," he said.

The young man smiled, and the old man grinned wider and took the stranger's hand with both of his and shook it some more.

The boy who had been listening to the watch let go of the arm and pointed to the island. "Go to the *isla?*"

The young man looked across the channel at the island and nodded.

"*Vamos con mi papá,*" said the boy.

Another song was playing. A boy wearing a pair of white B.V.D.'s started to dance in front of the bench.

"Are these all your children?"

The old man smiled and, twisting his body to the

music, took the stranger by the elbow down to the beach, where the duffel bag was being set into an old dugout canoe.

The children pushed the boat out into the shallow water with the dark boy kneeling inside, bailing with a rusted coffee can. The old man eased himself over the back edge of the canoe and sat down, picking up a red rubber bulb from the gas tank and pumping it. With the baby propped across her hip, the pregnant woman waded into the water, her knotted umbilical cord pushing its shape through her dress. Behind her in the sand the girl waited, covering her mouth and nose with both hands, crying.

The young man took off his tennis shoes and socks and rolled up his pants to his knees and splashed into the water. Chips of wet wood broke off in his fingers as he crawled over the side and knelt in the gasoline and grease in the bottom of the canoe. The engine started, and he sat down and put his shoes and socks in his bag. The boy dropped the coffee can in the sludge and went up and crouched in the bow. As they swung away from the beach, the old man slid a ciga-rette out of his shirt pocket and lit it, flipping the match between the stranger's feet. The old man winked and lifted his face into the wind, exhaling a stream of smoke.

On the shore the children picked up small pieces of coral and hurled them at the boat and chased after each other behind the pregnant woman. The young man slung a hand over the side of the canoe and rubbed his face with saltwater. He wet his lips. He looked across the channel at the island, where a row of pink and yellow houses lined the base. A patch of palm trees marked one end of the row; a low flat building on a sandy peninsula marked the other. Long green bungalows trailed off around the flat building and down the beach.

Among the houses towered a great white church, and below the church a cement pier fingered out into the water. From under the awning of a black and red schooner, a column of black men unloaded crates and stacked them on the pier. Smaller boats and canoes rocked in the water offshore or rested on the beach in front of the houses.

Around the reef at the peninsula, more green bungalows appeared behind the flat building. The jungle sloped up the mountainside and a beach filled a cove. The old man steered with one hand and dragged on his cigarette. He jerked his head toward the island.

"Why you go there?" he shouted.

"The hotel's my parents'."

The old man cocked his head sideways and raised his eyebrows. The wind lifted up his collar on one side.

The stranger cupped a hand around his mouth and leaned forward. "My parents own the hotel. It's my parents' hotel."

"My parents' hotel," said the old man. He pinched another drag on his cigarette and flicked the butt in the water, veering the canoe toward the shore and up alongside a wooden pier in front of the low green building.

The stranger got out with his bag and gave the dark boy a dollar. The old man revved the engine and spun the canoe away, raising up a hand and touching a finger to his forehead, down to his stomach and across his chest from side to side. He turned and stared back at the island, racing the canoe out the cove with the dark boy curled low in the bow, the old man's pants legs and the American dollar flapping in the wind.

3

The planks of the wooden pier rumbled and the stranger turned around to see a chubby man in red shorts and an orange flowered sports shirt running toward him, waving his arms in the air and shouting. "Señor Roger. Señor Roger. It's you? You are so late, señor."

The fat man slowed to a walk and stopped in front of the duffel bag, reaching for the young man's hand and huffing. "I am waiting for two weeks, señor. We are out of food and liquor, and the guests are wanting to leave." He let go of the hand and wiped his sleeve across his forehead. "You are Señor Roger, no?"

"You're Pepe?"

The fat man wiped his forehead again with his other sleeve. "Sí, señor. I am Pepe. The bartender, the guide, the bellboy, the bell *capitán*, the translator, and the chef. Welcome to Isla Grande. But we must hurry." He reached down for the bag. "The shit is hitting the fan."

Roger stared at the fat man.

Perspiration rings mushroomed out from under the armpits of the orange shirt, and a bald patch glistened on top of the sweaty head. Pepe straightened up with the bag. "The guests, señor. We are out of the liquor, and the Canadians are not happy."

"What about my parents?"

Pepe set the bag down and blotted his forehead with the front of his shirt. He shook his head. "For more than three weeks now." He nodded at the low flat building. "The hotel is killing me."

A wave lashed through the posts under the empty veranda. Across the far side of the railing, palm trees arched in the wind.

"Please, señor."

"My parents have a house?"

"They have a room. But nobody's there. Only the furniture and the clothes."

"Where?"

Pepe sighed and picked up the bag, shaking his head and turning around. "Nobody's there. It's a dead horse you're trying to kill."

Roger followed the fat man down the path, curving around the side of the low building to the row of green bungalows facing the water. Pepe climbed up the steps of a bungalow and set the bag down on the porch, unlocking the door with a key clipped to a brass ring on his shorts. Inside, he rolled up one of the blinds and looped the string around a nail. Roger stood in the doorway and looked at the room.

"It's the same as all the time," said Pepe.

Roger took a few steps inside.

"I'm in the city to buy the supplies. When I come back, nobody is here. Nobody but the clothes."

Roger sat down on the bed and stared at the photographs on the dresser. "They went somewhere?"

"Not with the *turistas* coming. Where they going to go with no clothes?"

"You told the police?"

"The *guardia*? Sí, señor, But there's nothing to do. There's no crime. And in Panama the people are always missing. It's a place of the easy come and the easy go."

A breeze blew through the open door. The doillies hanging over a pair of armchairs stirred.

"Who else was here?"

"The maid."

"No guests?"

"Sometimes nobody is here for a long time."

"The maid didn't see them?"

The fat man shook his head. "One day, sí. But the next day, no. She comes in the morning." He looked down at the bag on the floor. "You will stay the night in this room? I have the one on the other side for you, near to the water."

Roger lay back on the mattress and folded his arms across his chest.

"It's a terrible thing. I'm going to name my son, the next one, the same as your father. A beautiful name, no? Benjamin. Benjamin Antonio Leopoldo Mosqueda de Vaca."

The murmur of waves falling on the beach echoed through the room. Roger turned his head away from the door.

"I go to the restaurant," said Pepe. His footsteps crossed the room and stopped. "And if it's a girl, señor, I'm going to call her Benjamina. Benjamina Antonia Leopolda Mosqueda de Vaca."

The door closed.

Roger rolled over on the bed. A sliver of plaster cut his cheek. He brushed it off the bedspread and closed his eyes, smelling the perfume and cologne in the sheets.

4

With the moonlight streaming through the window onto the bed, he awoke in a chill. Perspiration beaded his neck; sweat thickened his hair. He rubbed his hands across his face and stood up, wandering in the dark toward the door. He grabbed the handle and turned it. The door stuck. He jiggled it against its jamb and worked the handle again. Leaving it, he walked through the light to the window and felt around the edge of the screen with his fingertips. He beat on a corner with his fist until the aluminum band snapped away from the wood and the screen swung up.

Roger crawled through the opening and out onto the front porch. Smoke darkened the beach. Dozens of white figures knelt in the haze, heaping sand into piles, poking holes in the middle of the domes, planting candles, striking matches. Flickers of light pulsed on the ground. The smell of sulfur filled the air.

A black woman in a white dress that shined in the light stood up in front of the veranda. Her hands clutched lighted candles; wax caked her fingers. Roger stepped off the porch into the sand, and the woman charged him, hurling the sticks against the bungalow and running down the path into the jungle, screaming. The people on the beach turned their heads toward the noise and came out of their crouches. The aluminum screen flew up and clanged against the window casing in the wind.

He went toward the main building of the hotel and up the steps and into the empty restaurant, where Pepe balanced on a stool, hanging glasses over the bar.

"What's going on out there?"

The fat man looked out through the windows. He hung the last glass and climbed down, mopping an apron over his face and walking toward Roger at the door. "*Macumba*," he said. "The magic of the black."

"One of them threw candles at me."

Pepe poked his head out the doorway. "It's only the people from the town, señor." He latched the screen and closed the door, setting the dead bolt. "But it's better to be safer than more sorry. Sometimes they drink the blood of the chickens and talk with the dead. The things I don't understand, I think it's better to give the shadow of the doubt."

Pepe softened his voice. "Like God. I never see Him, but I don't want to make the mistake and go to the Devil, so I think maybe it's true. Some things are hard to understand, no, señor?"

A breeze through the cracks around the door puffed against Roger's chest. The beach glittered in the window.

"You were sleeping?"

He nodded.

"Then you are hungry. When I sleep, I can eat a donkey." The fat man patted his stomach and chuckled. He peered out the window and waddled toward the kitchen.

Roger went to a table at the front of the room and sat down. Pits of yellow candlelight dotted the beach. Pepe brought a bottle of red wine and poured a glass, leaving the bottle on the table. Roger took a sip.

On the window in front of the table, a hand holding a piece of tallow clawed at the glass, smearing a white cross. The woman from the bungalow pressed her nose on the windowpane and glared into the room, her nostrils steaming rings on the panel, her gums sparkling with saliva.

He grabbed a box of matches, cracked it off the window, and skidded his chair back, getting up. The woman darted away. Wisps of vapor clung to the glass below the cross. He moved to another table and sat down with his back to the beach and drank, refilling the glass.

Standing between the salt and pepper shakers, a folded piece of paper read:

WELCOME TO ISLA GRANDE.
WE HOPE YOU ENJOY YOUR STAY IN PARADISE.

YOUR HOSTS, Ben and Birdie Lord

A wave on the beach hit the pilings with a splash
and ran up under the restaurant floor, hissing in the
sand and going silent. Flames from the candles on the
beach fluttered across the wine glass. He turned the
card face down and picked up the glass, propping his
elbows on the table and resting the cool rim against his
lips.

5

A group of tourists chattered in the far corner of the restaurant, toasting each other and taking flash pictures.

Pepe leaned over Roger's table in the back of the room. "Señor, you do not want the fried banana or the rice and the beans? And the fish without the others is like the dog without the bone."

Roger blinked at him.

"Or maybe it's the Canadians who say that." Pepe reached across the table and nudged a saucer of dark mush and yellow wedges. "You do not want the desert, señor? The black banana and cheese?"

Roger shook his head.

"It's very good for the stomach."

"Just the wine, Pepe."

The fat man stacked the dishes and silverware on a

tray and rattled toward the kitchen. The plate glass windows quivered as a wave rumbled against the wooden beams under the veranda.

A slap jolted Roger's shoulder, spilling wine from his glass and over his fingers. "You're Ben's son."

A bony man gripping the neck of a bottle and a shot glass in one hand pulled out a chair and sat down. He wiggled out a pack of cigarettes from the front pocket of his shirt, tossing them on the table and squinting at Roger. "You look just like him. Always at goddamned attention."

His bottle banged on the table. He swallowed the liquid in the shot glass and wiped his mouth with the back of his hand. "I'm Dutch." He set down the glass. "You must be Roger."

Roger dried his fingers with a napkin and they shook hands.

"My boat's out there." The bony man pointed toward the cove. "Next to what's left of your old man's." He refilled his glass, sloshing the tablecloth. "Water down here eats through wood like termite piss. Ever seen termite piss, kid?"

"They've got a boat?"

"Looks like acid. Got little brown shit floating in it. Splinters and sawdust and shit."

"Where'd they get a boat?"

"Had it when they got here."

"I didn't know they had a boat."

"Didn't know they had a son." Dutch raised the shot glass to his lips and tipped back his head, swallowing once and sliding the glass onto the table.

"You know what happened to them?"

"Disappeared." Dutch weeded a cigarette out of the pack and hung it between his lips. "Happens all the time down here."

"What happens?"

"Disappearing."

"Just disappearing?"

"Like booze."

"They just vanished?"

"Gone. *Sayonara. Adiós amigo.* Ever busted someone's cherry, kid?"

"What about the police?"

"The *guardia*?" He lit the cigarette and threw the match on the floor. "They couldn't find their own turds." He took a drag and blew the smoke into the air and leaned forward. "Unless you paid them. Then they'd find them. They'd be shitting all day if you paid them."

"You have to pay them to work?"

"They'll work. They just won't find nothing unless you pay them."

"That's blackmail."

"That's Panama, kid."

Pepe stopped a few feet away from the table, wringing his hands on his apron and looking at the bottle of wine. "Señor, the Canadians are still thirsty." He tilted his head toward the people in the corner.

Roger handed him the bottle.

"Thank you, señor." The fat man pressed it against his stomach. "We are out," he said. "Out of wine. Out of food. Out of money. Out of everything."

"What money?"

"The money. For the hotel. For the food."

"Don't the guests pay?"

"Sí, señor. Before they arrive."

"Everything?"

"Except the drinks."

"Then you have some money from the bar."

"No, señor."

"Don't you sell drinks?"

"No, señor."

"You don't sell drinks?"

"Sí, señor."

"Pepe, you sell them or you don't?"

"He gives them away," said Dutch.

"You what?"

"Sí, señor."

"You give them away?"

"What can I do? The *turistas* are here and they're thirsty, and when Señor Ben is not here, I don't have the money for the change. There's nothing to do. And the Canadians are the most thirstiest people in all the world."

"Why don't you write down their names and how much they owe? Then they can pay later."

The fat man stared at Roger.

"You just give them away?"

"Sí, señor."

"Free?"

"What is the hotel without the drinks?"

Roger picked up his glass of wine. "Okay. Tomorrow. We'll do something tomorrow."

"Thank you, señor." Pepe went away with the bottle

toward the laughter and the flashing camera.

"Why doesn't he just write it down?"

Dutch's bottle clinked against the rim of the shot glass. "Can't write. Most of them down here don't finish school. Lots of them don't even go. You can't eat books for Christ's sake."

"Then who wrote the letter?"

"He spoke. I wrote." Dutch raised his glass and emptied it into his mouth, licking the overflow off his bottom lip. A stream of liquid dribbled through the stubble on his chin.

"So what am I supposed to do here?"

"Have another drink."

Roger looked through the window at the moon rising over the ocean.

"Have some of mine." Dutch poured from his bottle into Roger's glass.

"How do I find my parents?"

"You speak Spanish?"

"No."

"You don't speak Spanish. You're three thousand miles from a cop. You don't know nobody. You don't know Panama. People disappear down here like piss in the ocean, kid. Maybe they'll come back. Maybe not."

"Why not?"

"I don't ask why."

"Then why'd you write the letter?"

"I didn't write the goddamned letter. Pepe wrote it. You're their son, aren't you? He can't run the hotel."

"I can't run it. I don't want to run it."

"Well, shit, kid." Dutch stood up and tugged at his

pants. "I gotta take a piss." He staggered toward the kitchen door.

Roger took his wine glass and went outside to the veranda. He sat down on the edge of a chaise lounge. Moonlight stippled the reef and coned into a point near the shore. Spray floated in the air as a crab skirted across the wet deck.

The bony man walked out the door and over to the railing, filling his shot glass and looking down at the beach. He threw back his head and poured the drink into his mouth.

"Out here, kid, what you don't know might hurt you, but what you do know can kill you." He turned to Roger. A wave lapped the pilings. "I've been here five years. I get more stupid everyday."

"You don't want to go back to the States? Don't you have a family?"

"Kid, you can piss your whole goddamned life away. Or you can get on a boat and cut the lines, and end up in the middle of Madagascar, or Fiji, or Isla Grande for Christ's sake. I'm sixty. I don't want to die in some stinking rest home. I want to die at sea. Ever been at sea, kid? At night?"

"No. I just did some day sailing."

"If there's a moon out, like tonight, you can see the wind blowing across the water. Even when there ain't no moon and you don't see nothing, you feel it. The boat comes down off a wave like you're flying. You learn faith. You can't sail and not have faith, kid. And you can't feel that in the middle of goddamned Kansas. All those people out there in those places like that,

they're all lost 'cause the land's there, and their feet
tell them that everything's okay. But it's not okay, kid.
People are nuts."
   "That's why you like sailing?"
   "I like it 'cause it's free. I got no taxes. I take my
house with me. I catch my own food. I get on and off
when I want, and I can leave when I want."
   "You don't like people."
   "I don't worry about what they think."
   Roger took a sip from his glass, shivering as he
swallowed. "So where you going next?"
   "Tierra del Fuego. Land of Fire. Ever heard of it?"
   "I think so."
   "Down at the end of South America. You know why
they called it that, kid?"
   Roger shook his head.
   "Well, when Magellan sailed through, it was blowing like a whore's lips on an army payday. And cold.
Cold as an Eskimo's tit. They didn't know exactly
where in the hell they were in the first place, 'cause no
one'd ever been there before. At least, no one they'd
ever heard about. So they sailed through into this windy,
bear's ass of a passage down at the end of the goddamned world half-expecting to fall off, and the son of
a bitch got dark." Dutch took a drink from his bottle
and pointed at the sky. "And then, all of a sudden, up
along the cliffs they saw these huge fires burning from
the Indians who lived up there in the mountains. And
the wind was thumping and howling against the sails,
but they knew they weren't alone no more.
   "Then they got back to Europe and told everybody

about it and handed out maps, and more people came
over and brought horses and shit like that and decided
it'd be a nice place to live. So they told the Indians to
go fuck off. And now there ain't no more fires in the
Land of Fire. You just got the goddamned name. That's
the way the world is, kid. People are nuts."

"So why you going there?"

"I told you. Imagination. Ernie the Hem. Willy the
Shakes."

"Who?"

"Hemingway, kid. Shakespeare." Dutch swigged
from his bottle and stumbled down the stairs and onto
the beach. "Have another drink," he called, unzipping
his pants. "I gotta take a hell of a piss."

6

Birds screeched. An alarm clock ticked. Roger rolled over on his back and pulled a pillow across his face. Someone rapped on the door.

"Señor Roger. You are awake?"

He lifted up the pillow.

"Señor Roger. I have the girl. The maid."

He turned on his side, hugging the pillow against his stomach. "Five minutes."

The doorknob clicked.

"Five minutes, Pepe."

"Sí, señor."

Water slushed across the sand outside the bungalow. A shadow roamed back and forth in the light under the door. Roger inched his legs to the edge of the bed and let his feet fall to the concrete. He stood up and staggered into the bathroom, leaning a hand on the wall over the toilet and flushing the handle. He peed into the bowl.

Wiping his face with cold water from the sink and raking his fingers through his hair, he went back into the front room and pulled on his pants. He fastened the buttons on his jeans and opened the front door. Sunshine burst into the room and struck his chest.

"Good morning, señor. Are you shipshape?"

Roger rubbed the heels of his palms across his eyebrows and down the sides of his face. A girl in a pink dress sat cross-legged in the sand with her hands folded on her lap and her dark skin gleaming. She rocked forward on her knees and stood up. A red bracelet fell around her wrist.

"The maid," said Pepe. "Moonshot."

Roger stepped off the porch and sat down on the beach. Pepe nodded at the girl and she sat down again. Drops of water hung in the springs of her hair. Her neck and shoulders shined. Pepe sat in the sand between the girl and Roger.

"You were here when my parents disappeared?"

The girl nodded.

"When did you see them last?"

"It was on a Wednesday morning, when I was leaving. Mrs. Birdie was working in the garden and Mr. Lord was helping her. I said good-bye and I went home."

"That's it?"

She nodded. A droplet slipped off a curl of hair, fell onto her collarbone, and trickled down her chest, soaking into the pink cotton around her breasts.

"You didn't see anything?"

"No. The hotel was empty. The next day I came back in the morning. When the guests leave, Mrs. Birdie always gives me something to do. I couldn't find her. I waited for a long time, until the afternoon. When I knocked on their door and called their names, they wouldn't answer. I went inside. It was late in the afternoon. No one was there."

"You told Pepe?"

"The next day, when he came back from the city."

"How long were you gone, Pepe?"

"Two days. I leave on Tuesday in the morning, and I come back on Thursday in the afternoon."

"You always take two days?"

"Sí, señor. It's a long way, and I have the wife in the city and the one in the country."

"Two wives?"

"Sí, señor." Pepe unbent his leg and stretched it out with the other one. He leaned back on his palms.

Roger wiped both hands over his face. "Sometimes there aren't any guests?"

"Sí, señor. The ones today leave tomorrow, and more are coming in three days. But we don't have the food and the liquor."

"Who collects the money?"

"Gloria," said Pepe.

"Who's Gloria?"

"The one who collects the money. She lives in the city. She's the cat's payamas."

"Pajamas?"

"Sí, señor. The cat's payamas."

Roger picked up a handful of sand and sifted it between his fingers. "My parents keep any money here?"

"There's the safe in the office. Maybe it's empty and maybe it's full. It's the six of one and a half-dozen of the others."

"Can't you just speak regular English, Pepe? You know where Gloria lives?"

"Sí, señor. I'm speaking the regular English. She lives in the city."

A swarm of black butterflies flitted across the beach, weaving into the trees behind the bungalows. Roger stood up and brushed off the back of his pants. He looked at the girl and then at Pepe and took a deep breath and forced out the air.

"I didn't bring any money with me. I can't pay either of you. And I can't buy anything for the hotel. We can try the safe, or maybe this Gloria can help, but I can't run the hotel. I don't know anything about it. I just want to find my parents."

"How you going to find them?" said Pepe.

Roger turned and walked toward the water.

"But how you going to find them?"

He walked into the water to his knees and bent over and wet his face and neck with his hands. A man hunkered on the reef with a blue net lumped across his shoulder.

"There are two kinds of people," said Pepe, walking to the water. "The people to think, and the people to do. The people to think have the easy life, but it's always short. They live like the funny joke, and then they die. It's because the ideas are always changing.

But the people to do, they live to see many children
and the children of the children. The people to do have
the hard life, but it's always long. It's because the
work, she always stays the same. You understand,
señor?"

"No."

"If they come back, we will be happy. But what are
they going to do if we don't have the hotel?"

The man on the reef sprang up, flinging the blue net
from the ends of his fingers, the corners unfolding in
the wind and falling on the water. Roger pushed a hip
through a swell and fell forward, turning on his back.
The sun bleached the sky white; clumps of green trees
stood pillowed along the mountain ridges. He peeled
off his jeans and lobbed them up on the beach and
dipped his head back, filling his ears with water. He
floated and nibbled salt off his lips.

Something moved at his side. He turned his head
and lowered his feet. A fin circled in the water behind
him. He heard the girl's voice. He tried to run, flailing
his hands at the ocean and lunging toward the shore.
The creature surged in front of him, grating its tail
against his thigh and swimming past. Roger dove,
crawling through the surf and falling onto the beach on
his back. His chest and stomach heaved; urine dribbled
down his leg. Pepe and the girl stood over him.

"Shark," he said.

Pepe slapped his hands together and laughed. "I
never saw one so close. And then he doesn't take
nothing. Maybe he doesn't like the smell. Maybe he
wasn't hungry."

The girl dropped his pants in the sand. "Dolphin."

"What?"

"It's better we are men and not small fishes, no señor?" The fat man shook his head and chuckled. "The *delfín*."

Roger turned onto his stomach. A wave slashed over his legs and up his spine and down, sinking his body into the sand. Plovers on the beach drilled their beaks in the foam. The gray fin humped in the water and dove in front of the reef.

"It's the trick of life, no?" said Pepe. "To have danger when there is nothing, and nothing when there is something."

Roger pushed himself to his knees, grabbing his jeans and stumbling into the ocean.

"You will help with the hotel?"

He sat to his shoulders in the water and touched his thigh. "You think my parents will come back?" he shouted.

"With the help of God, señor. But if God does not want it, who are we to say no to Him? *Hay muchos caminos en la vida.* Many roads in life. It's better to be happy with the road in the banana trees. Then all the roads are good and there is nothing to make you sad. I'll go to cook the lunch, señor."

Pepe and the girl started away, then stopped and turned around. "Señor," called Pepe. "Would you like some fish for lunch today?" He hooted and shook his head and strolled down the beach toward the hotel, the girl's red bracelet dangling from her hand.

7

"Sure you know what you're doing?" asked Roger. Dutch slouched back in a folding chair and waggled his palm on the top of his bottle. A smoldering cigarette hung between his lips.

"Why don't we move back a little?" said Roger.

Dutch took the cigarette out, raised the bottle up to his lips, and drank, flicking his tongue at the opening as he gulped. He put the bottle down on the ground and picked up the end of a wire, sparking it with the tip of his cigarette.

"Too damned wet." He flipped the cigarette butt to the side and dropped the fizzing wire in the dirt as he picked up his bottle and rocked back against a tree.

Down the back steps of the hotel clattered Pepe, watching the spark move along the ground while he ran over to the two men. "Señor Roger. Señor Dutch.

What you doing?"

"Blowing up the goddamned safe," said Dutch. He plopped the chair down and stood up, taking a swig and raking his hairy chest with his fingernails. He walked toward the building.

"What is it?" said Roger.

"I don't hear nothing," said the fat man.

The three climbed up the back stairs and into the hotel office. Smoke hovered near the ceiling; sticks of dynamite decorated the safe.

"Wet as a whore's cunt," said Dutch. He hitched up his pants and walked between Roger and Pepe, bumping against the door jamb and staggering outside and down the steps.

"After lunch," called Roger. "Let's do it after lunch."

Dutch swung the bottle away from his body and let it fall back against his leg as he walked, hooking a finger through a belt loop and hauling up his pants above the crack in his ass. He turned the corner.

"Is he always like that?" said Roger.

"Like what?"

"Drunk."

"Sometimes I find him sleeping on the beach like this." Pepe bent his arms in the air. "Like a dead bird. But the other times it's like this."

"Drunk or passed out."

"It's the way he is," said Pepe.

They walked into the dining room and Roger sat down at a table fronting the water where the glass louvers clinked in the wind. The edge of his paper napkin fluttered over the ends of a knife and fork. He stared at the ocean; whitecaps scarred the cove.

Pepe set a plate of food on the table.

"The lunch, señor. The beans, the rice, and the fish. I caught it in the morning from the pier. An ugly fish, no? But the taste is okay with the chili."

Roger looked at the fish and picked up his fork and took a bite.

"It's all right, señor?"

"Hot."

"Good for a long night with the women."

Roger took a glass of water and drank, refilling the glass from a pitcher.

"Sit down, Pepe."

The fat man pulled out a chair. "The water is okay? It's from the mainland."

Roger nodded and took another drink.

"On the island the taste is like the ocean. So we bring it from the mainland for the *turistas*."

Roger set the glass down and ate some rice. "How long you worked here, Pepe?"

"Since last Christmas, señor. My cousin was working in the kitchen. Pelé. It's Carlos, no? But we call him Pelé because he loves *fútbol*. You know Pelé?"

"A soccer player?"

"He doesn't play now. He's too rich and too old to play. It's why the name is so funny. My cousin, he is very poor, and he runs like a chicken. But the Americans like baseball, no?"

Roger took a bite of fish and nodded.

"It's good, too. But soccer is better. It's more like life. So much work for so little points."

"What happened to your cousin?"

"Maybe he went to Colombia. Maybe Costa Rica. His wife found him so he has to leave."

"He's hiding from her?"

"No, señor. Running."

"Why doesn't he get divorced?"

"Ah, señor. You don't go to church? If he divorces her, he cannot go to heaven. It's better to go to Colombia."

Roger took a bite of rice and beans and another drink of water. "Does everyone speak English around here?"

"Sí, señor. Except for the *guardia*. But he is like me and speaks English, too."

"But isn't this Panama?"

"Sí, señor."

"Then why don't they speak Spanish like on the mainland?"

"You don't know the story?"

Pepe scooted his chair closer to the table and wiped his hands on his apron. "It's a long time ago when *los negros*, the blacks, are living in the country of Florida. There is fighting, and they have to leave in the boat. It's a flat boat with nothing on the side and nothing on the top."

"A raft?"

"I think so. They travel for many days and many weeks. It's a long way, and some of them get married, and the women have babies, and there is always dancing and the *fiestas*. They love to dance, no, señor? But none of them is a doctor, and some of the babies die

in the sun. And you know what happens next, señor?"
Roger put a forkful of beans in his mouth.
"They eat them."
"What?"
"They are very, very hungry. After a long time of
having the babies and dancing and eating, maybe one
year or more, they find the island of Isla Grande. Even
today they like to make babies and dance. Some people
say they still eat them, but I do not believe this. And
they keep the English to now. I think English is so
difficult they don't want to forget and have to learn all
over again."

Roger set his fork on his plate and reached for the
water. An explosion and a gush of air and plaster from
the back of the room threw him into the table and onto
the floor. Chairs crashed on their backs and sides,
table legs splintered apart, glasses shattered. A cloud
of gray smoke gusted across the room toward the
windows as hunks of wall crumbled to the floor.

Roger shoved Pepe off his leg and stood up, sweeping powder from his arms and pants. Through the
mangled wire and plasterboard, palm fronds thrashed
in the wind behind the hotel. Dutch's bottle rested on
the chair in the shade.

Roger and Pepe clambered through the wall of the
office and down the back steps of the hotel. Liquid
feathered across Roger's lip. He scraped a knuckle
under his nose and wiped off blood.

"What the hell are you doing?"
"Shit," said Dutch. "Will you look at this?"
"You trying to kill us?"

Dutch kicked a board off a pile of rubble and reached into the safe lying on its back in the dirt. He pulled out a bundle of paper money. "Bingo."

Roger bent closer.

"Sure as hell ain't the bar money," said Dutch. "You seen this before, Pepe?"

"Only in the movies, señor."

"They're hundreds," said Roger. "All hundreds. Where'd it come from?"

"Maybe is stolen, or maybe is being stolen," said a voice from behind them.

The three men turned around to face a thin man chewing on a toothpick. Green fatigues sculpted his crotch and thighs and tapered below his knees into the tops of his boots. Across his chest the stenciled black words SARGENTO DE LEÓN smudged his white T-shirt.

"*Sargento* Vicente Francisco Martinez de León, *La Guardia Nacional*," said the man. He nodded at the money in Dutch's hand. "Where is it from?"

"From the safe," said Roger. "In the wall."

With his shiny black boots crunching over the chips of broken cement, Sergeant de León walked over to the stairs. He leaned inside the office and worked his toothpick into a corner of his mouth. "In the wall?"

"Yes," said Roger.

"You do not have the key, señor?"

"My parents didn't leave the combination. I'm their son."

The sergeant stepped away from the building and walked back over to the mound of debris, propping his right wrist on the knob of his holster and tucking his left hand behind his back.

"The money and papers will be held as evidence," said the sergeant.

"Evidence for what?" said Roger.

"The explosion, señor."

"For Christ's sake." Dutch tossed the bundle of money back onto the pile. "Didn't you hear it? I'll get my camera. You can take a goddamned picture."

The sergeant unstrapped the cover on his holster and drew the revolver, slamming it against the bony man's skull and dropping him to his knees. He jammed the end of the barrel into Dutch's ear. "You will give me the money, gringo?"

Pepe knelt down in the ruins and scraped up the bills.

"It's my parents' money," said Roger. "I'm their son. You can't just take it. They're coming back."

A trickle of blood ran down the side of Dutch's face. The sergeant chomped on his soggy toothpick and smiled. "We will see," he said. "We will see."

8

The jeep swerved around a troop of ducks in the middle of the road and slid down an embankment, struggling back up the side and onto the gravel again. Pepe stuck an elbow out the driver's window and steered with one hand. The jeep faded to the right, and he yanked it back into the middle of the road as Roger braced his hands against the dashboard.

"Where first, Pepe?"

The jeep roared off the gravel and onto a section of asphalt, swaying around a pothole and throwing Roger into the door.

"First to the company of *turistas* for more money. Second for the food and the drinks. And third . . . ." He turned to Roger and grinned. "The third is Consuelo for me and somebody nice for you. No, señor?" The jeep thundered into a pit and skipped onto the shoulder and back down to the road.

The pavement switched to clay and then gravel and then back to asphalt as they passed miles of hills, barbed wire fences, and trees. Here and there around a curve, a collection of shanties appeared, guarded by rusted cars and dogs lying in the dust. Scattered columns of men with machetes plodded along the ditches on the side of the road, burlap bags full of firewood slung over their shoulders.

Across a bridge the jeep stopped and turned left onto a highway. Telephone posts lined the road, wires dipping from pole to pole. Between two hills the jungle divided. A white freighter sailed toward a lake.

"The Panama Canal," said Pepe, "is like an empty coconut. The general, the first one to do something, said the Americans were taking all the money." He nudged Roger on the shoulder. "It's okay with me. You dig the hole, no? But the general said this is no good. He told the Americans to leave. But still we never see the money. And now the canal is falling to pieces."

"Why don't they fix it?"

"How?"

"I don't know. Don't they know how?"

"For the parts we need the money, no?"

"Then where's the money?"

Pepe shrugged his shoulders. "This is the problem. In Panama we can never fix nothing. We can only go to church and pray."

The white freighter disappeared behind a levee, and the jeep wound through a marshland staked with cattails and tall grass and shacks under the trees. A convoy of netted trucks came toward them and passed, the charcoaled faces of soldiers peering out from under the tarpaulins. Behind the transports trailed cars and buses, honking their horns.

"Carnival," said Pepe. "Already the people are leaving. It's only Wednesday."

"Leaving for where?"

"The people from the city go to the country, and the people from the country go to the city." He laughed. "But the *guardia,* they go everywhere, no?"

Roger turned around and watched the passing line of camouflaged trucks. "They look like soldiers."

"They're like cockroaches. The small guns are the police, and the big guns are the soldiers. But it's all the same. It's the *guardia.* Like cockroaches, they are everywhere."

Pepe turned off the highway and entered the city. Shadows from the apartment buildings darkened the avenues. Rainbows of clothes flapped from the balconies and out the opened windows. A group of shirtless boys chased a tin can in front of the jeep, clanking the container into a gutter and cheering. Sitting on the trunk of a parked taxi, two men scraped mango peels across their teeth and ogled the women waiting to cross the street. Helmeted soldiers at the intersections waved on buses and cars and smoking motorcycles.

Pepe parked behind a fruit cart straddling the curb. The hum of voices mixed with the sound of brass music and the shuffling of feet. A hawker, clanking a string of pots and pans around his neck, thrust a bag of popcorn through the window of the jeep. Roger shook his head. The man glared at him and went away.

Pepe took a coin out of his pocket and gave it to Roger as a boy's hand, reeking of excrement, reached through the window and opened and closed in front of Roger's face.

"For him." Pepe nodded at the boy. "He's going to watch the car."

"The car? What for?"

"So it's here when we come back, señor."

Roger handed the coin to the ragged boy, and he squeezed it in his palm and backed away from the door, picking at a scab on his face. Roger and Pepe got out and joined the mass of bodies swarming the sidewalk.

The crowd flowed around an armless man, sitting inside a toy wagon, painting on a canvas with a brush crimped between his toes. The brush nipped at a swirl of white paint on the edge of a broken platter. The foot lifted, swinging to the canvas, melting a highlight into the eye of a condor, brushing patches under the opened wings. The man's chest heaved as he worked, his bottom lip trapped beneath his tongue, the sleeves of his shirt pinned closed. Pepe dropped a coin in the wagon, and they walked around the corner.

Roger followed Pepe through a gold-tinseled doorway to a stairwell. A woman with metallic red lips stood at the bottom of the stairs. She watched the fat man pass and raised a leg in front of Roger, slamming her spiked heel against the wall and blocking his path.

"Excuse me," he said.

She gathered her skirt and scrunched it down between her legs. "Sucky sucky," she said.

"What?"

"Fifty dollars. Two times." Tobacco stains marked her teeth. A sore bled on her lip. She reached for his belt, and he grabbed her wrists and walked around her.

"No, thank you," he said. He held out his empty palms. "No money."

They climbed up the flight. Music blasted through the walls; a fluorescent tube twittered on the ceiling. At the top they walked down a dim hallway, stopping in front of a nameplate marked GLORIA TRAVEL. Pepe pushed the buzzer beside the door and turned the handle.

Inside the room a woman in red sat behind a desk, talking on the telephone. She smiled and waved them in with gold bracelets jangling on her wrist. Pepe nodded, and they walked over to two chairs in front of the desk and sat down. An air conditioner chugged in the window; a poster of Egyptian pyramids trembled in the stream of air against the back wall. From a drawer in her desk, the woman slipped out a bottle of perfume and sprayed her neck, smiling at Roger. She hung up the phone and flounced her hair.

"Pepe." She clipped a gold earring onto her ear and extended a hand. "*Qué sorpresa.*"

The fat man stood up and bowed. "Gloria, this is the son of Señor Ben and Mrs. Birdie, Señor Roger."

Roger reached across the desk and shook the woman's thin fingers.

"He's so handsome." She gazed at his chest as he

and Pepe sat down.

The fat man cleared his throat. "Gloria, we have a problem."

Her nylon stockings whistled as she crossed her legs. She fixed her eyes on Roger's mouth. "Your parents are not back?"

"Not yet."

"I was for sure they went away and then came back. But, no?"

"No."

She trilled a clicking noise with her tongue. "*Qué pena*. It's a great pity." She picked up a gold cigarette case from her desk, letting her bracelets chime together.

"The money from the tourists comes to you?" asked Roger.

"It's my job." She chose a cigarette and inserted it into a cream-colored holder and placed it between her lips. Pepe leaned forward, taking a gold lighter and lighting the cigarette.

"Is there any way we can get some of it? An advance? We're out of supplies for the hotel. And I don't know how long I'll have to be here."

Her lips parted. Smoke eddied out of her mouth. "You're staying in town tonight?"

"I guess so."

"Then I'll get the money and find you a nice hotel."

"I think Pepe already has a place to stay."

"And you? You have a place, too?"

"Me?" Roger looked at Pepe, who was looking at Gloria.

She smiled. "It's okay then. I know all the best places. I'll call the bank."

She rested her cigarette in an ashtray and picked up the receiver and dialed. Reclining in her chair, she stroked the gold chain that hung around her neck and rubbed it between her lips. She smiled and spoke into the phone.

Pepe turned to Roger and winked. "Hot payamas," he whispered. "No?"

9

The drive spiraled through the hills above the city, past royal palms and spired gates, down streets with new curbs and fresh blacktop, past mansions overlooking the sea. In the drizzle the red sports car skidded around a corner and onto a boulevard along the coast. High-rises lined the road with marble, teak, and tinted glass.

They stopped in a parking lot at the back of a cul-de-sac, beside a building inlaid on its side with the words La Tortuga in jade. Gloria and Roger got out of the car in the rain. He carried his bag.

"It means The Turtle," she said. Her keys tinkled in her hand as she walked, her red heels clacking across the concrete. "Not a good name for someplace to live, no? Who wants to live inside an animal, especially a slow one?"

A man in a tan uniform sat perched in a chair in front of the building. He gripped the handle of an umbrella that belled over his head. Pressed to his ear, a transistor radio slurred out Spanish.

"*Goooooolllll*," screamed the radio. "*Goooooolllll*."

Static crackled from the speaker. The man in the uniform tipped his chair down onto the cement and held the umbrella high over the walkway as he opened the front door. He caught the bottom of the rosewood door with his toe and rushed the radio back up to his ear. His eyes sparkled. Goose bumps pebbled his arms.

"*Fútbol*," said Gloria with her heels clicking louder as they entered the building. "*Fútbol, fútbol, fútbol.* Soccer, no? The game of the peasants. You only need the ball to play or sometimes only the paper bag. They love it."

Terrazzo checkered the floor. Wrought iron benches surrounded a fountain, water dripping into a basin with silver coins quivering on the bottom. Gloria pressed a button on the wall. The elevator opened and they got on.

"This is a hotel?"

"My home. But it's like a hotel. Birdie and Ben stay here many times, and I have many rooms. It's only me and the servant." Gloria smiled and fingered her key ring as the elevator rose. "But she can't see."

At the tenth floor the door opened, and they walked into an alcove walled with mirrors veined in gold. Gloria unlocked a glass door, and a breeze fanned her hair back. He followed her in and set his bag down on a wicker chair. A papaya tree stood in a bucket beside a love seat; a cluster of fruit hung at the top of the trunk. Around the end of a sliding glass window, drapes swirled into the room and out onto a veranda.

"You like some fruit?" She took a chalice of plums and bananas from the dining table and offered him the bowl. He chose a plum, and she called through a double door in Spanish. A woman answered.

"We'll go outside." Gloria set the bowl down and unfastened her high heels, pitching them onto the love seat and walking barefoot across the tiled floor. She stopped and pointed to a picture on the wall. "It's me. You like it?"

He looked at the smiling portrait. A spotlight from the ceiling softened the naked shoulders and spread a sheen across the chest, into the dark areolas, up the erected nipples. Her breasts mounded forward and to the sides. Two shadows swept down to the ribs.

Gloria fondled her breasts with both hands and raised them. "It's the plastic inside, no? But the look is real." She smiled like the photograph. "The feel is nice, too."

Roger took a bite of the plum and trailed her out onto the veranda. A stream of purple juice dribbled off his chin. At the handrail he looked down and ate. Seabirds squawked; rain streaked the air. A wave slammed over a crag of rocks, tangling kelp around a log inside a tide pool.

"Over there is the entrance to the canal," she said. "And out there, the ships are waiting to go in." She took the plum out of his hand. "Sometimes I think they stay there forever." With her teeth she peeled away the skin from around the stem and nibbled at the pulp. "Sweet, no?"

Flaring her lips, she slipped the pit and two fingers into her mouth, closing her lips over the second knuckles, tightening her cheeks, breathing through her nose, easing out the stone to its tip and sucking as she stared out at the sea. She jerked forward, dripping liquid out her mouth and away from her dress. With a finger she caught the stream, licked it off, and swallowed.

"*Aquí, María,*" she called. "*Estamos aquí.*" She pulled a chair over to the rail and dropped the pit over the ledge.

Roger dried his hand on his pants and sat down on the edge of a hammock.

"When she knows where you are," said Gloria, "there's no problem. But if you're silent, she's like a drunk Mexican." She laughed. "Sometimes I play with her like I'm dead. It makes her very angry and she breaks many things. Sometimes, she breaks so many things that the money she gets is all gone, so I give her some of the dark bananas." Gloria shook her head and rubbed her tongue over the juice stains on her fingers.

The servant crept onto the veranda with two glasses and a pitcher tottering on a tray. Ice cubes smacked each other in the liquid; spoon handles rang against the rims of the glasses.

"*Limonada,*" said Gloria. "How do you say it in English? I forget."

"Lemonade?"

She nodded. "Lemonade . . . and a little rum."

Gloria took the tray from the servant. "*Gracias, María.*"

"*De nada,*" said the old woman. She wiped her hands on the front of her uniform and turned around, eyelids frozen open, eyeballs bulging. One of the strings on the hammock hit her head, pasting her hair up on one side. Gloria laughed, and the old woman smashed down her hair and shuffled away.

"It's no good to laugh," said Gloria. "But it's funny, no?" She poured a glass of lemonade. "Now, tell me about you."

"Me?"

She handed him the glass. "All about you."

"Like what?"

"Like how old you are."

"Twenty."

"And what you like to do?"

"I don't know." He took a sip. "I like sailing. I like to swim. I got a scholarship for swimming. And I like movies."

"Me, too. I like the bang-bang, the cowboys. It's exciting. It's good to have excitement, no?"

Roger swirled his drink.

"What else you like?"

"History, I guess. It's my major in college."

"Ah, the history is very old. I like the young more. The old is dead, and the dead never makes you happy." She guided her glass to her mouth with both hands and trapped an ice cube with some lemonade and rum, swallowing the drink and dropping the ice cube back into the glass with her tongue. "And the girls, Roger? You like the girls?"

"Sure." He removed the spoon from his glass and

drank.

"You're married?"

"No."

"And children?"

"No," he said. "I'm not married."

"It's good. Me, too. My husband is dead." She patted her chest. "The heart. I wake up in the morning and he was blue. I push and push and he just stays there, like he was dead. It was horrible. I can't sleep in that bed. I give the bed away and change the room and still I can't sleep." She took Roger's glass and added more lemonade and poured another glass for herself. "Sometimes, life is shit, no?"

"No children?"

"Not for me. But for Tony. In Panama the man can have two families if he's careful and has the money. Crazy, no? I saw them at the funeral. It was the first time. Now I decide that life is too short and I'm sorry for the past. I take his money, and I buy this apartment and the two plastics." She touched her breasts. "And I have the business." She finished her drink and smiled. "He was a bastard."

A bell tinged from the living room. The last red rays of the sun filtered through the clouds on the horizon. The sea, speckled with white water, darkened.

"Time to eat," said Gloria.

Inside, she turned on the stereo and lit a pair of white candles on the dining table. She switched off the lights. They sat down to a table of china and crystal on a lace tablecloth. A saxophone purred between cellos and violins and the high pinging notes of a piano. A wire brush swished across a cymbal. Gloria squirmed her body to the music.

"I feel like dancing," she said.

The servant backed out of the double doors from the kitchen, wavering toward the table with a steaming bowl.

"She's pretty good to carry the soup," said Gloria. "It's with the wine she has the trouble. Can you do it?"

The servant found the table and set the tray on the edge, ladling out two bowls of soup and shambling back through the swinging doors. Roger poured the wine from a carafe.

"How long have you known my parents?" he said.

"From the time they came. Maybe two years ago. They came from the San Blas."

"What's that?"

"The San Blas Islands. It's not far from Isla Grande. It's very beautiful. But the Indians make everyone afraid."

"They have Indians?"

"The Cunas. They are so small these people, but very angry. They hate the hotels and the *turistas*. And especially they hate the soldiers. I think it's okay now, the soup." Gloria sipped from her spoon and nodded.

Roger spread his napkin across his lap. "Why don't they like anybody?"

"They're primitives. It's hard to teach people like these, no? Even the missionaries are afraid."

He stirred his soup. "How often do you see my parents?"

"Maybe every month I go to the island. This week-end I'm going for Carnival. And there's a man coming who knows your father." Gloria slid her fingers up and down the stem of her wine glass. "Maybe you can stay here for a few days and drive me to the island. The road is so bad to drive alone."

Roger scalded his lip on the soup and poured more wine.

After dinner they slow-danced as her thumb sat curled inside his palm and her breath warmed his ear. She tripped on his feet and giggled, brushing a line of saliva off her bottom lip and pillowing her cheek back on his shoulder. She nested her stomach against his groin.

The servant crept into the room and slipped her hands up the candlesticks, snuffing out the flames with her fingers and fumbling with the plates in the darkness. A red button glowed from the stereo. A piano was playing with a flute.

"Roger, you do it more from the front or the back?"

"What?"

"You never do it before?"

He moved her hair away from his nose. "Do what?"

"Love," she whispered.

"Make love?"

"Yes. Make love." She danced slower.

"If I do it from the front or the back?"

"You never do it?"

"I guess the front."

"I like it more with the back upside down and the front around. You know why?"

"No."

"It's like flying. You like to fly, Roger?"

"I guess so."

"Making love is also like a dance because you have to count. Like the cha-cha. The cha-cha-cha in the airplane. But you don't have to count if you don't want to. Sometimes I count and sometimes I forget to count. I love to dance." She burped and kissed his neck.

"Tell me about my father," he said.

"You don't know him?"

"He was in the army until I went to college."

"You were in the army, Roger?"

"No. My father."

She nodded against his shoulder. "When they came to Isla Grande, they only had the boat. The owner of the hotel doesn't want to stay. It's too far from the town, and the road is so bad. So the owner gives your father the hotel and tells him to pay something for every month."

"Why'd they come to Isla Grande?"

Her hand uncoiled from his fist and cradled the back of his neck. She tongued his ear and nuzzled her breasts into his chest. "Sometimes life takes us, and we just follow."

She lifted her head and looked at him with glazed eyes. Her forehead fell against his nose, and she sagged in his arms. He dragged her to the sofa and laid her down, covering her with a blanket from a bedroom. He turned off the stereo and went outside to the veranda and sat down in the hammock. Red and green ship lights glowed through the bars of the handrail. A plate crashed in the kitchen, and the blind maid began to cry. The city twinkled in the rain.

10

Roger squatted on the toilet with his legs spread, grunting. The water ker-plunked. He took a deep breath and exhaled, reeling off a string of toilet paper from the roller and wadding it in his hand. He stood up and reached back. The bathroom door opened.

"*¿Señora?*" The blind maid peered around the corner, pinching her nose and souring her face. "*Ay, señora. A la mesa.*" She backed out and shut the door.

He dropped the paper in the bowl and flushed the toilet, pulling up his pants.

In the living room, Gloria slept on her side on the sofa with the blanket dumped on the floor and the sunlight flooding in from the veranda. Roger took a croissant and a slice of papaya from the dining table.

"*¿Señora?*" said the maid.

He stuffed the end of the roll into his mouth and

grabbed his bag, sneaking to the front door. Gloria stirred.

"*¿Señora? ¿A dónde va?*" called the maid.

He opened the door and crept out, closing the door behind him and pushing the button for the elevator. The servant wandered after him, gawking through the glass. "*¿Señora? ¿Señora?*"

He ate the bread and fruit in the elevator on the way down and tossed the papaya skin in the can outside the entrance of the building, where in his chair the door-man slept. He walked across the parking lot and out onto the boulevard.

A cloud of vapor rose from an open manhole. Horns honked. Jaywalkers dashed through a maze of cars and buses. Drivers swerved their vehicles from lane to lane. At the corner he joined a crowd of people waiting beside a lamppost and took out a piece of paper from his pocket.

As a bus slowed to a stop, he inched forward with the crowd, up the steps of the doorless vehicle, and inside. Felt balls dangled from the windows. Music trumpeted out a speaker nailed above the door. Painted angels flew on the ceiling. The bus roared its engines and lurched ahead, throwing the passengers together. A hand wiggled through the crowd and grasped Roger's forearm. He yanked his arm away and whirled around to a boy standing beside him.

"My watch. Someone took my watch."

The boy tilted his head to the side and yelled in Spanish. The driver halted, and the boy vanished through the crowd. The bus jarred forward again.

Two school girls stared at Roger from the aisle, chewing on gum and pushing up their breasts with notebook binders clasped to their stomachs. A girl with a hand on an old woman's shoulder nodded toward him as she whispered in the old woman's ear. Grappling his bag over a man, he found a seat next to a cracked window. He turned to the man and tapped his wrist. "Someone stole my watch."

The man extended his arm and peeked under his white sleeve. "*Son las siete,*" he said, holding up seven fingers.

Roger leaned his head against the cold glass and rubbed his wrist. The bus stopped and started as shoulders bobbed to the rhythm of the music and a finger thrummed against the back of his seat. The bus turned a corner, passing a block of rusted tin shacks. Children banded naked beside a shed, showering under a spigot in the mud, soaping their heads. Further down the street, bodies rolled in jackets and scraps of canvas filled the gutters and the merchants' doorsteps.

The bus parked in front of a row of vegetable bins and clothing stalls. The driver turned off the engine and got off. Roger paid a man at the rear door of the bus and walked down the steps and into a marketplace crowded with women and children and old men. An adobe chapel stood in one corner of the square. He walked across the plaza and into a dark opening in the side of the church.

A group of shadows sat huddled against the back wall. Light trailed in from the doorway and over the dirt floor to a table with a cross and two unlit candles.

Roger clutched his bag in one arm and held out his paper to a woman suckling a child near the door.

"Excuse me. Can you tell me how to get to this address?"

The woman stroked the back of the baby's neck.

"Can I help you?" A bald priest in a brown robe walked into the light.

"Are they sick?"

"Maybe," said the priest. "You're a doctor?"

"No."

The priest nodded at the woman with the child. "She lost her children, except for the baby, when they attacked her village."

"Who?"

"The government? The rebels? Each says it's the other."

The woman rocked forward and back against the wall, gazing at the gold cross on the priest's chest.

"You're a tourist," said the priest.

"No."

"A Catholic?"

"No. But my father was. Before the war."

"War takes away the faith of many. I was a chaplain in the Canadian Air Force."

Roger looked at the dark altar and the unlit candles.

"My father parachuted into some trees. Someone climbed up and cut him loose. He was killed coming down."

"Your father?"

"The other soldier."

The priest shook his head.

"So after that he became a Jew. The soldier who saved his life was Jewish."

The priest nodded. "So you're Jewish?"

"When I was younger."

"Then you're here on business."

"I'm looking for my parents. They disappeared from their hotel about a month ago."

"There is so much darkness in the world," said the priest, touching his cross.

Roger showed him the paper. "Do you know where this is, Father? I think I took the wrong bus. They stole my watch."

The priest looked at the paper and pointed out the door. "Take bus 5. It's out front. Get off after you pass the second cathedral. It's not very far from there."

"Thank you, Father."

"Good luck with your business," said the priest. "And don't worry about the watch. You have your life, and time stopped in Panama many years ago."

Roger thanked the priest again and walked through the marketplace, boarding bus 5 in front of the square. He pushed his way down the aisle, grabbing onto a handle on the back of a seat. A large black woman in tight pants brushed up against him, her fleshy hip bouncing into his, her breasts ballooned in her sweater. The bus jumped forward and swung through the streets, stopping and starting. The crowd of people blocked his view of the buildings. He showed the woman the paper.

"*Aquí,*" she said. "*Estamos aquí.*"

"What?"

"*Parada,*" shouted the fat lady. "*Pa-ra-da.*"

The bus jerked to a stop, swaying the passengers into each other. The fat woman nudged him toward the rear door. "*Esta aquí. Aquí.*" She pointed out the window.

Roger gave the man at the turnstile a coin and squirmed through the crowd to the door. A half-dozen hands searched through his pockets and shoved him into the street. He stumbled to the sidewalk, reaching to his back pocket as the bus belched smoke and sped away.

"You bastards," he yelled. "You slimy bastards."

A woman with a child cocooned on her back turned around and held out her hand, limping toward him with her eyes hollowed in her skull and her cheek bones bulging. "*Americano,*" she whispered. "*Americano.*"

11

PANADERIA CONSUELO read the sign at 316 Avenida de las Americas. Roger climbed the two broken steps and went inside. Sunlight glared between the slats in the wooden walls. The floorboards creaked. Around the room hooked a cabinet filled with rolls, blue flies crawling on the inside of the glass doors. A light bulb dangled from the ceiling by a cord.

A girl wearing a red scarf around her head wrapped a few rolls in a sheet of pink paper. She handed the bundle to an old woman who dropped a coin on the cabinet and scuffled away, stuffing the bread into a canvas bag hung on her forearm. The girl looked up at Roger and reached behind her head, retying her scarf, her blouse pressing across her breasts and lifting them.

Roger massaged his wrist. "Pepe?"

The girl wrinkled her brow.

"Is Pepe here?"

She went to a doorway at the back of the room, putting her hands on her hips and tilting her eyes up toward the ceiling. She shouted in Spanish and a child answered. Footsteps pounded down a flight of stairs. Around the corner, munching on a roll, appeared Pepe. "*Hola,* my friend. You found it the easy way?"

"Someone just stole my wallet," said Roger. "On the bus."

"It's not Panama unless they steal your wallet."

"And my watch."

"You're getting off on the wrong side of the bed." He glanced at the girl and stuffed the last of the roll in his mouth. "And how was the lady, Gloria? She made you happy?"

"Why don't we call the police?"

Pepe brushed the crumbs off his hands. "They only come if there's a dead body or someone to shoot. Now the watch is gone, and the money is used for a thousand things." He lifted up the counter board. "Come. Meet my family. Then we go."

Roger walked past the girl and followed Pepe through the doorway, up a narrow flight of stairs, and into a large room above the bakery. Several children wrestled on the floor inside the room. Cots lined two of the walls. Along another wall five stoves led into the kitchen. A thin girl in torn shorts slid a tray out of an oven. Her nipples puckered through her T-shirt, sweat trickled down her neck.

In a side room, a large woman lay sprawled across a mattress on the floor, her head propped on one arm.

A portable television droned, and children sitting on piles of clothes around the set turned over scraps of bread in their fingers and watched a black and white cartoon flickering on the screen.

"This is Consuelo," said Pepe.

The woman, gnawing on something in her mouth, looked up at Roger. The flab jiggled on her chin. She blinked and turned back to the TV.

Pepe clapped his hands twice and up from the floor and out the room scurried the children. They lined up by size, laughing and pushing, the tallest one standing under the fat man's outstretched arm. The noise and the fidgeting stopped, and Pepe lowered his hand and strolled down the line.

"Here is Fernando . . . Felipe . . . Francisco . . . Mario . . . María. These two are the same."

"Twins?" said Roger.

"But not really the same. This one," he squeezed the chin of the boy and winked at him. "This one is smarter." The big-eared boy grinned. Pepe placed both hands on the girl's cheeks, kissing her on the forehead.

"And here is Franco . . . Oscar . . . Jorge . . . Marta . . . Carlos . . . and Anna. Beautiful this one, no? Like a flower." Pepe bent over and smooched the smallest girl on the nose. She giggled and scratched her face.

"And in the kitchen is the oldest, Lucía."

Thin Lucía looked up from the ovens and wiped her neck with a mitten.

"So many," said Roger.

"It's like a birthday all the time, no?" He clapped his hands and the children scattered. "We go."

In the bedroom Pepe knelt down on the mattress and nibbled at the woman's neck. She squealed and swiped at him with her hand, and he scrambled away, jeering at her in Spanish and chuckling.

The children waved and shouted as the two men went down the stairs and through the store. They passed the girl in the red scarf at the doorway.

"The cousin of Consuelo is selling the bread," said Pepe. "A virgin."

They got into the jeep and drove away as the girl leaned against the bakery door, tightening her scarf. Her nylon stockings hung bunched around her ankles; her black leather shoes glared the same color as her eyes.

The jeep turned a corner and a box tipped over in the back, rolling a can against Roger's foot. He picked it up and looked at the label.

"French mushrooms?"

Pepe swung the jeep around another corner and grabbed at his crotch. "Good for making love. We trade them with the Colombians."

"You trade mushrooms?"

"For anything you want. Rum from Puerto Rico. Cigars from Cuba. A radio from Korea . . ."

"Mushrooms?"

"Sí, señor. Everything."

"With Colombians?"

"A good business, no?"

Roger put the can in the back. "My father knows about this?"

"Sí, señor." Pepe nodded several times. "He knows."

Through a maze of crowded streets they drove until the buildings grew smaller and cardboard shacks led them out of town. A dog pranced along the road, clutching between its teeth a rat, the tail swinging from the dog's mouth. The city ended and they followed a road cut through the trees.

The jeep turned off the highway and climbed into a range of green hills, twisting around the side of a mountain and into a valley. A river wound beside the road; the sound of water rushed below. Monkeys jabbered. A donkey jerked a wooden cart through a field. They entered a town and parked the jeep in front of a house with high white walls and green double doors.

"You coming inside, señor?"

Roger shook his head. A pair of girls strolled down the sidewalk arm and arm, staring at the jeep as their high heels clopped against the cobblestones.

"Is there anywhere to eat?"

"Near the corner. The beer is warm, but the soup is good." Pepe reached under the seat and took some money out of a cardboard box. "It's better if you keep it in your shoe." He handed Roger the bills. "And keep your feet on the ground."

They got out and Pepe went into the house. Roger wandered up the street behind the two girls, who turned back, looking at him and whispering to each other. A taxi drove by with the driver leering out the window and whistling. A dog nosed a lamppost and lifted its leg.

Inside the restaurant, Roger sat down at the end of a row of nicked tables and chairs stretching along the wall opposite the bar. A girl with a lavender dress that swished when she walked swayed down the aisle, slipping a menu and a glass of water on the table. She waited, hip cocked, lips pinched together on one side of her mouth.

"I'll have a bowl of soup and an ice tea."

"¿*Cómo?*" said the waitress. Mascara glued her eyelashes together in bunches. She cocked her hip to the other side.

"A bowl of soup and an ice tea."

"¿*Sopa?*"

He nodded. "Soup."

She scooped up the menu and swished away, returning with a steaming bowl and a rolled-up paper napkin and plunking them down on the table.

He unwrapped the napkin and a spoon clanked out onto the table. He picked the utensil up and stirred the broth. Moisture dribbled down the sides of the bowl; pieces of red sausage bobbed in the liquid. The girl passed again and Roger held up a finger. "Could I have an ice tea?"

"¿*Cómo?*" said the girl, cocking her hip.

"An ice tea."

She strode down the aisle and came back with two pieces of white bread on a plate and set them beside the napkin.

"Ice tea," he said. "Tea with ice in it."

She dipped her head sideways and looked at the soup.

"Not soup. Tea." He put the spoon in the bowl and cupped his fingers, moving them up to his mouth and down and back up again. "T . . . E . . . A. Something to drink."

The girl frowned and left, returning with a bottle of orange soda and a straw. Roger took a drink and dipped a slice of white bread into his soup. The waitress wiggled up on a bar stool, where she lit a cigarette and wrapped her feet around a leg. Her toes tapped against a rung.

The barkeeper bent over the bar and whispered something in her ear. She flicked her ashes on the floor and shouted at him, and he slapped a towel over his shoulder and backed away from the counter, raising his hands and laughing.

The men at the bar leaned forward on their elbows and smirked. The waitress stood up and swatted one of them across the shoulder, and the men coughed with laughter and made sucking noises with their lips as she strutted down the aisle, the outline of her panties showing through her dress.

Roger finished his soup and paid the bartender. With the rest of the money in his shoe, he walked back to the car. Telephone wires drooped between the houses. A red kite hung in a tree.

When the door to the white house opened, a boy poked his head out. Pepe came over to the jeep and got in as another head appeared below the first. The fat man started the engine and waved to the faces as he drove away.

"It wasn't too long? It's always busy." The jeep jerked over the cobbled street.

"How many do you have?" asked Roger.

"Nine. And one more almost ready."

"So that's how many altogether?"

"Together . . . it's thirteen . . . and nine . . ."

"Twenty-two?"

"And maybe one more next month." He turned a corner and flipped on the radio.

"Don't you worry about them?"

"Worry, señor?"

"You have so many."

"It's natural to have children, no?"

"But what about the Church?"

Pepe tapped the steering wheel to the beat. "I go to church every Sunday."

"The Catholic Church?"

"Of course."

"And the priest doesn't say anything?"

"The priest?"

"Because you have two wives."

Pepe danced his shoulders to the music. "I have two priests."

"But wouldn't they say it's a sin?"

Pepe reached over and turned down the volume. "A sin, señor?" He stared at the road as the jeep roared off the cobbles and onto dirt.

"Does God love everybody the same?"

"Yeah, I guess so."

"And aren't the children everybody?"

"Yeah."

He turned to Roger. "Then God will forgive them because I have the two wives and the two families and the two happinesses."

"But what about you?"

"Me?" Pepe put a hand on his chest and smiled. "Me, señor? I will forgive them, too."

"And my father?" said Roger. "My father has two families?"

"It's always possible. All you need is love and a way to do the two things at the same time. Keep the right hand behind the left. There are some men who have enough love for three families. Good, no? All the world is trying to kill us. But the man with many children, he never dies. He always has somebody to take his name."

Pepe gazed down the road, jiggling with the rumble of the jeep. "Wouldn't you like it, señor, if you could live forever like my Uncle Nico, who already makes love with all the women in Panama, half the women of Costa Rica, and some of the women of Nicaragua? Every boy in the city of San José has a nose like my Uncle Nico." He slapped Roger on the shoulder and laughed, turning up the radio and singing with the background singers in the band.

12

Across the channel from Isla Grande, a group of children swarmed around the jeep as it splashed through a row of mud puddles and stopped behind the shacks facing the island. Pepe climbed out with a box of candy, tearing off the top and setting the carton on the hood of the car. Roger helped him unload the food from the back of the jeep and carry it to the skiff while the children loped down the sandbank behind them, sucking their candies and crackling the cellophane wrappers in their fingers.

On the passage to the island, the sun burned the back of Roger's neck. Bags of oranges and potatoes buckled the sides of the cracker tins. Pellets of sea water sprayed over the bow. Entering the flat of the cove, the boat slowed and drifted toward the wooden pier. Two boys in white underpants caught a line from

Pepe and tied the skiff to the dock as Roger peeled off his shirt, wiping the sweat and saltwater from his face. He lugged a box of food down the pier and up the steps to the hotel.

Inside the empty dining room a breeze blew through the louvers and shook the leaves of a hanging plant. A group of workmen sipping from bottles of beer lounged on the floor in the blown-out office. Roger gave the two boys a dollar and took out a beer from the refrigerator behind the bar. He rubbed the frosted bottle across his forehead.

The screen door in the dining room slammed against the wall, and Pepe stood in the doorway, holding a bag of groceries in one arm and pointing at the cove.

"The boat of Señor Ben is bleeding."

Roger rested the bottle on the bridge of his nose.

"It's making all the water white. Like a Christmas tree."

"What tree?"

"Like the snow."

"What snow?"

"The snow, señor. The boat is bleeding like the snow."

Roger took the bottle off his forehead and went to the window. Several sailboats sat anchored in front of the island. He twisted off the bottle cap and walked out of the hotel and down the beach toward the peninsula.

Heat wrinkled the air above the water as the sailboats lifted and set in the swells. Roger cupped his hands around his mouth and called out into the cove.

Dutch stood up in a dinghy, dangling a quart bottle at his side and waving his empty hand toward a sailboat. "Termite piss," yelled Dutch. White gel dripped from the hull of a derelict yacht.

Tossing the beer bottle in the sand, Roger walked into the water and swam out to the dinghy.

On board the leaking boat Dutch took a winch handle and broke off the lock on the main hatch. Roger followed him below, kicking a litter of clothes into the forward berth and picking up tools and clanging them into a stainless steel sink. Dutch dragged a mound of molded life vests up onto a table and rolled back the carpet from the floor. Kneeling on the floorboards, he removed a lid from the deck as Roger crouched down beside him.

"What is it?"

Water dribbled off Roger's knees and fell into the white bilge. He lay down and reached into the hole, poking a finger through a plastic bag and bringing up a lump of white powder. "Salt?" He touched it to his lips and squinted. "It's bitter." He nibbled his tongue. "And numb."

Dutch stood his bottle on the floor and lowered a hand into the pit, hauling up a scoop of the powder in his palm and flicking his tongue at it. He scraped his teeth across his bottom lip.

"What is it, Dutch?"

He brushed the extra powder off his hand and sat up, washing out his mouth with a drink and spitting into the hole.

"Cover it up, kid."

"But what is it?"

"Our asses."

Dutch took a long drink and stood up. He walked over to a row of cabinets, opening several of the doors until he found a jug and a plastic funnel. A pistol tumbled onto the counter top. Rattling the funnel into the neck of his bottle, he poured in liquid from the jug and shoved the gun back in the cabinet.

"Are you going to tell me?"

He added three glasses of water from the tap, removed the funnel, and held out the bottle, shaking it in front of his body. "Cocaine." He gulped down a swallow and took a glass, filling it half-full of drink and handing it to Roger. "Like the goddamned Gobi desert."

Dutch climbed up the stairs and Roger followed him into the cockpit, sitting down among the scatterings of hardened rope and rusted screws. A halyard banged against the mast as the boat sloshed from side to side. Dutch nodded toward the island and a black schooner floating at the pier in front of the great white church. A column of men ferried crates down a plank.

"See that boat with all the boxes on it? Fucking Colombians. Hijackers. They'll slit your goddamned throat and gut you like a fish. Then they'll throw you overboard. Sometimes they'll carve pictures on your belly or cut off your prick and use it as bait. One guy they found with a fishhook jammed in his mouth. Probably trolled him for a few days behind his boat until the line snapped. After they make their delivery, they sink the boat and go get another one. One boat, one trip."

"Drugs?"

He raised his eyebrows and nodded.

"You think they know about this?"

"If they knew, it wouldn't be here."

"Then where'd it come from?"

Dutch drank and wiped a trail of liquid off the side of his mouth. "My great-grandmother."

"You think it's my father's?"

"You can't count on nothing."

"He wouldn't do it. I don't believe it."

"Then don't."

"All that money in the safe came from this?"

"Who knows?"

"What do we do with it?"

"Nothing."

"Can't we get rid of it? Take it out to sea? Dump it somewhere?"

"You want to lose your pecker?" Dutch tilted back his head and guzzled from his bottle. "I'll patch up the hull. Nobody'll find it. The best thing is just forget it."

Roger sipped the drink and held the glass up to the sun. "What is this?"

"Alcohol and water, three parts to one. You're old man's recipe."

Roger threw the glass overboard and walked to the side of the boat. He stared down at the water.

"He's probably got the whole goddamned mast hollowed out," said Dutch, "and all the bulkheads crammed. That piece-of-shit hotel's been dragging ass for years. Something's got to pay for it."

"They're not like that. It's not theirs."

"Nobody's like nothing, kid. People are nuts, that's all. You can't figure it out if it don't make no sense to begin with."

Swinging his arms back and then forward, Roger dove.

"Kid," shouted Dutch, "you can't fucking count on nothing."

He raised and lowered one arm in front of the other and kicked his legs as the water rushed against his ears and garbled the bony man's words.

". . . remember . . . you . . . can't . . . fucking . . . on . . . nothing . . . count . . . on . . . nothing . . ."

13

In the morning, hands in his pockets, one bare foot falling in front of the other, Roger strolled along the shore as the water rolled up and wet his cuffs and ran back into the sea. He climbed a slope and squatted in front of a mound of sand with a pool of hard wax swirled in the center. The sound of steel drums beat through the palm trees. He reached for the wick.

"No, Roger." Moonshot scampered up the slope, lifting her skirt in front of her knees as she ran.

"It's out," he said.

"It's for the spirits." She bent down and repacked the sand around the candle and sat on the edge of the slope, folding her legs under her dress and looking out at the water.

He sat beside her.

"Your parents haven't come back?" she said.

"Not yet."

"Mrs. Birdie always gave me some work. Maybe one or two days a week."

"Aren't there other places?"

"Even in the city they don't have jobs."

"Then what do you do?"

"I must find something."

"Like what?"

"Something." She stared at the water. "There's a song my grandmother used to sing. It says there's no choice in thirst or hunger or loneliness. When we're thirsty, we can only find water. When we're hungry, we can only find food. And when we're lonely, we can only find love."

Roger crossed his arms on his knees and looked at the sand between his legs.

"I think it means we'll find the things we're looking for."

"What do you do?" he said. "For money."

"You don't know?"

She stood up and brushed the sand off her dress and walked away down the beach. He caught up with her and she slowed her walk. They passed the hotel and a garden and behind the last bungalows entered a grove of coconut palms with vines circling the tree trunks and ferns fanned out in the shade. Through the tunnel of foliage, light and shadow freckled the mud. The steel drums clacked louder; brass instruments tooted. The path burst into the sun.

Dancers and musicians paraded on a dirt road, drums tapping out the rhythm, trumpets and trombones hooting off-key. A row of stuccoed houses lined each side of the street. Old black men and women bouncing babies in their arms stood in the lime- and lemon-colored windows, watching. The percussionists taunted each other with twists and twirls of their sticks and spoons and clanging tin cans and cooking pots, challenging the dancers to follow, the dancers challenging each other to follow better.

A large woman in orange Bermudas led the procession of stuttering feet. The end of a red turban slapped her face with the jerks of her head. Her huge breasts slammed up and down inside her blouse while her swollen hands turned in the air, conducting. A bevy of dogs and prancing children straggled at her side.

"It's the last practice for Carnival," said Moonshot. "They're saving the best rhythms for tomorrow. And they aren't dressed today."

"Where do they go?"

"Up and down the road. You can walk it in ten minutes, but to dance it takes an hour. They'll make two trips today and maybe twenty tomorrow."

Into the town of two-toned houses they walked. Wooden shacks peered through the trees on the mountainside. Halfway down the road, the procession approached a pink and blue building with wire mesh tacked across the windows and a chain link fence lying on the ground. The leader stiffened a hand as she passed, saluting an empty flagpole in the sand.

At the pier at the end of town rocked a schooner, chaffing its side against a cushion of rubber tires. A circle of sailors played cards on deck and passed around a bottle. The black hull glittered in the water. Fuel drums cluttered the bow.

"Colombians?" said Roger.

The girl looked straight ahead.

The sailors drank and cursed each other and spit over the side into the bay. A man on the wharf hissed at Moonshot, stroking his hand up and down a bottle neck and shaking the bottle until foam bubbled out the end. He shoved it between his legs and hobbled down the pier toward the girl as the sailors on board howled with laughter.

Roger followed her across the street to the great white church and up the bleached white steps to the doors. A brass bell hung in the belfry; an iron cross spiked the roof. Half-open, the oak doors rested in grooves worn into the floor. They entered the alcove, where scraps of folded paper jammed the cracks in the stone walls, and the light dimmed.

Candles along the side aisles led to an altar with a gold cross. A man and a woman slumped forward in the first pew. In front of them a boy knelt at the rail below the altar, a hooded red figure looming above him. Two black hands rose out of the billowing red robe and clasped the boy's skull. A woman's voice echoed around the room, chanting.

Moonshot crossed herself and dipped one knee to the floor, and they sat in the middle of the church. A fold of her dress drooped across Roger's thigh.

The woman in the cloak lit a candle and placed it on the floor. She walked over with the boy to a portrait of the Virgin Mary and put him on his knees in front of the painting. Her hands fell on his head again. The voice murmured.

"What are they doing?"

"The boy's sick," said Moonshot.

"She's a priest?"

"A *mambo*. In our *macumba* she's like a priest or a doctor."

"But why are they here in the church?"

"To pray to the gods who live here."

The old woman lit another candle and placed it on the floor. She crossed in front of the altar to a painting of Saint Peter. The boy stood up. A line of polished red fingernails fell across Roger's shoulder. Lilac perfume pierced the air. A piece of jewelry jingled.

"So, you are in the church." Gloria's whisper blew into his ear. She leaned over and kissed his cheek.

The *mambo* wrapped her hands around the sick boy's eyes and pressed his head against her abdomen. The couple in the front pew turned and looked back at Roger. Gloria giggled, reaching across his face and putting a finger in each corner of his mouth.

She pulled.

14

The three walked out the door of the white church
and down the steps, Gloria sashaying alongside Roger,
her bracelets tinging. The Colombians folded their cards
and eyed the walkers as they crossed the street to the
beach.

"He's here," said Gloria.

"Who?"

"The friend of your father, Señor Robinson. He's
very worried, this man. You were praying?"

"Watching."

"Ah, it's very old, no? But they're older on the
mainland and ones with more gold. Some have all the
ceiling gold and the crosses gold and the cups. But the
most famous is the church with the gold table. So
much gold it hurts the eyes. It was the way to keep it
from the Spanish bastards." Gloria made the sign of

the cross on her chest. "The priests, they are not stupid, no?"

"No," said Roger. He looked back at the girl walking behind them. "Do you know Moonshot?"

Gloria glanced over her shoulder. "The servant?"

On the path back to the hotel, Moonshot vanished, leaving the branches nodding. Roger and Gloria continued through the jungle to the grove of palm trees, on past the bungalows, and up the front steps of the hotel. Inside the dining room a man with a black mustache and square jaw pushed his chair away from his table and stood up.

"Mr. Robinson?"

The man shoved a cigarette into his mouth and stuck out his hand. A diamond sparkled on his little finger. "Robinson Smith."

Roger shook the man's hand, and they sat down. Gloria called Pepe over to the table, her gold bands clacking across the arms of her chair.

"You have a Chi Chi, Pepe? In a tall glass?"

"We have the tall glass, señora, but we don't have the Chi Chi."

"Then I'll have champagne."

"Sí, señora."

"In the tall glass."

Pepe turned to Roger.

"An ice tea."

"It's Carnival," said Gloria. "It's not the time for ice tea. Have something to make you happy. Have some rum. Have tequila."

"I'll have a beer."

Pepe winked at Roger and waddled away.

Through the line of smoke twisting out the end of his cigarette, Robinson Smith squinted. He reset his drink on its napkin. "When did they disappear?"

"About a month ago," said Roger.

"No evidence?"

"Of what?"

"Of what happened to them."

Roger shook his head. "The safe was even full of money. I don't know why they'd leave."

From his pack on the table, Robinson Smith shook out another cigarette and put it in his mouth, lighting the new one with the old.

"How long have you known my father?"

Smith crushed the butt in the ashtray. "We joined the army together. Fought in Korea. After the war, he stayed in. I ran into him down here a couple of years ago."

"Señor Robinson is a great *aventurero,*" said Gloria. "Like your father."

"Spanish galleons," said Robinson Smith. "They're all over the place down here."

Pepe brought a collins glass of champagne, a beer, and an empty glass and set them down on napkins on the table.

Gloria raised her drink. "A toast. To the gold."

Robinson Smith inhaled on his cigarette.

"My father's been treasure hunting?"

"He does the diving. He's got all the equipment and that old Grand Banks."

"What Grand Banks?"

"That white powerboat anchored in front of town."

"I thought he only had the sailboat."

Robinson Smith picked up his drink. His ring chimed on the tumbler. "He bought it off of some Colombian, I think."

Roger filled his glass with beer. "You think the money in the safe was from something you found?"

"How much is it?"

"I'm not sure. The *guardia* took it."

The man with the square jaw stared out the window and smoked.

"We've got an agreement, your dad and me, not to talk about it except between ourselves. I know you're his son and everything . . . ."

"It's interesting," said Gloria. "No?"

Robinson Smith stamped out his half-smoked cigarette in the ashtray. "We were going out this weekend. I guess I'll have to find somebody else."

"You're not waiting?"

"This time of year you can't wait around. *Chubascos* are coming. Too many rain squalls." He tilted back his glass and finished the last of his drink.

"Well," said Gloria, "this weekend I'm free, and I'm a lucky girl. You know why?"

Roger picked up his beer and watched Robinson Smith over the rim as he drank.

"Because I have the two most handsomest men in all the island, and it's Carnival. Maybe your parents are going to return for the dancing and the music. They say anything is possible in Carnival. Maybe I'm going to get married. Who knows?" She lifted the glass of champagne to her lips, and her bracelets shimmied to her elbow.

With his pack of cigarettes in the same hand, Robinson Smith clicked his lighter and lit another cigarette, his
nostrils turning orange in the flame. He stood up. "You'll
excuse me. I've got some things to do before tomorrow." He shook Roger's hand and left the room.

"You want to dance?" said Gloria. "I have the music
in my room."

Roger set down his glass and refilled it, watching
the foam creep over the side and down. "Maybe later."

"Tonight?"

He got up and walked over to the bar with his beer.
Pepe dumped a pair of frosted glasses into a sink of
water.

"Hot stuff," said the fat man, nodding at Gloria.
"No?"

"You know that guy, Robinson Smith?"

Pepe lowered a pitcher into the basin. "I don't like
him. This is the place for a good time. It's not for
business."

"He's my father's friend?"

"Sometimes they take the old boat with the big
engine and put on the tanks and the boxes and go out
in the ocean. But they never come back with anything,
and they never have a good time. It's not like friends
to me." He drew a glass from the scalding water and
set it on the counter.

"They never find anything?"

"I never see nothing. They come back and they never
get drunk or laugh. It's too serious. It's not a vacation.
It's the same like work, no?" Pepe stacked the pitcher

and more glasses on the counter.

"Where do they go in the boat?"

"They leave before the sun and come back at night. But they never say where they go."

"How often?"

"Maybe one time a month. Sometimes two."

Pepe plunged a hand into the water and tore out the plug. The water gurgled. He dried his hands on his apron and smiled. "But tomorrow, señor, is Carnival. The day for everyone to have a good time."

"What happens tomorrow?"

"First, the guests arrive from the mainland. All the rooms are full, and the restaurant and the bar are like the day I win the lottery. When the sun sets, the parade begins and then the parties and the drinking and the dancing. Everyone is drunk and fighting and making love. It's the one day we wait for in all the year." The fat man massaged his pudgy fingers with a towel.

"It's a religious holiday?"

"Sí, señor."

"For what?"

"For what, señor? For the Christ, and for God, and for everybody. It's the time to feel happy before the sadness."

"Sadness?"

"Sí, señor."

"What sadness?"

Pepe flipped the towel over his shoulder and leaned forward, pressing his belly against the sink. "The sadness, señor." He looked into Roger's eyes. "You mean, you do not know about the sadness?"

15

Flinching at leaves as they brushed across his face, Roger tramped through the moonlight toward the town, bodies flashing ahead of him on the path. Wood and metal click-clacked a running beat. A light shone through the bushes at the edge of the jungle. Where the path met the street, he shaded his eyes from a bank of floodlights. A portable generator chugged nearby. Sparklers in the hands of children sealed the town with haze. Firecrackers exploded. Crowds of people watched a parade.

Scores of dancing drummers filled the road, rapping on copper pots and tambourines, their sticks and knuckles blurring. Some of the drummers had boots with strands of beads slapping against the sides. Others wore spats, or silver slippers, or strips of colored cloth wrapped around their feet. Medals pinned to shirts glittered next to sequins and fluorescent buttons. Long streaming ribbons flip-flopped from the ends of the twisting instruments.

All along the parade girls danced inside circles of drummers as the men closed the pockets with a loud rhythm and then crept away, softening the beat. The girls, in shorts or bikinis dusted with gold and silver speckles, humped the rhythm back with their hips, their breasts, their thighs.

A thin man with a trombone and a white tuxedo and top hat commanded the brass musicians, who marched in twos and threes, kissed girls, and drank from bottles thrust at them by the crowd. The thin man kicked up the tails of his coat and raised a gloved hand in the air, and the men released the women and jabbed their horns to their lips. The band played.

At the head of the procession promenaded the kings and queens and dukes and duchesses, trailed by their attendants and dancers, weaving in and out among them. The attendants wore three-cornered hats and white knickers and carried the trains of the queens and duchesses and the capes of the kings and dukes. With glass stones twinkling in the bulbs, the royalty toted jeweled scepters, pumping them as they walked. A king stepped out in front of the others and twirled on his heels. A duke jumped up and smacked his ankles in midair, landing flat-footed on the ground and returning to his stroll.

A small boy dressed as an attendant led the parade. His legs wobbled to the beat, almost collapsing under him as he spun across the street, leaning left, then right, dropping to his knees and rising straight up on his toes and strutting out ahead of the royalty, bending his body backwards and lifting up a hand, fluttering it in the air, every movement in time with the brass and the sticks and the ringing tambourines.

On both sides of the road, in front of the houses, on the rooftops, in the trees, people danced and drank and sang. Young children sat perched on taller shoulders and threw yellow wildflowers and mimosas and purple orchids in the street.

"Some party," said Robinson Smith.

Roger turned to the man smoking at his side. Fireworks lit the sky.

Gloria squeezed between Roger and Robinson Smith, locking an arm around each man's elbow and rubbing her hips against theirs as she gyrated to the pulse of the music. Red rhinestones and blue quartz studded the bodice of her see-through dress.

"Let's go," she said, pulling them into the crowd.

Waving a bottle and singing, a man with a patch over his eye swaggered up to Gloria. He lifted up his patch and winked at Roger and handed the bottle to Robinson Smith. Gloria danced into the center of the parade, quivering her body under the sticks of a group of men in green-striped pants whose silk shirts hung open to their waists in sweaty V's.

From across the street, Moonshot waved. Roger pushed through the crush of people to the other side of the road.

"You were dancing?" she shouted.

"It's hard to follow."

"Because you don't try."

He laughed and took her hand and pulled her behind the houses to the beach, where a group of boys sat on crates, tapping out a rhythm with spoons on chips of porcelain plates. The boys sang. A wheelbarrow churned through the sand, clay bottles with corks in their mouths chinking against each other in the cart. A woman bought four and set them at the feet of the boys.

"What're they singing?"

"The song of Carnival," said Moonshot.

"There's only one?"

"The most famous one. 'Do you hear the drums of Carnival? The night of Carnival has come. Do you hear the rhythm of Carnival? Come and dance with me. Carnival is here and we are whatever we want to be.'"

At the shore the water blinked with lights. Roger and Moonshot walked over to an overturned canoe and sat on the hull. Women and children crouched in the tide, watching the lights in the cove. A guitar played. A man was singing.

"They make boats from paper," said Moonshot, nodding at the women, "and put candles inside for the spirit of someone they love. A boat that carries its candle out to sea will reach its owner and bring him peace."

The candlelighters stooped over bags bunched on the sand. The women struck matches and held the candles as the children caught wax in the paper hulls. With the candlesticks set, the women carried the boats into the water, floating them at arm's length and nudging them forward with their fingertips. Glowing through the paper, the orange and yellow lights drifted toward the pier or capsized in a ripple.

"They don't go very far," said Roger.

"It's the current."

"Why don't they make them out of wood?"

"They have to be paper. Wood is too easy."

"Then it's luck."

"Maybe," she said.

Through the smoke that shrouded the beach, a woman in a white dress slipped toward Roger and Moonshot.

"She's the one who threw the candles at you," said Moonshot. "At the hotel."

The woman crept closer.

"She thinks you're Mr. Ben."

The woman stopped and stared at Roger. Her eyes widened. She wrinkled up her face and spit between his feet, then backed up toward the water, glaring.

He shoved himself away from the canoe. "She's crazy."

"She's showing you she's not afraid."

"I'm not Ben Lord," he shouted at the woman. "I'm Roger." He tapped his chest. "I'm his son."

The woman scowled and spit again and ran down the beach.

"I'm his son," he yelled.

A gust of wind collared the paper boats and pushed them toward the shore, spilling them in the surf.

"She's crazy."

He took Moonshot by the hand and drew her onto

the road strewn with flowers, past the hordes of revelers awaiting the parade's return, past the drunken men urinating on the walls, past the showers of confetti falling in the dust, to the empty path and the tunnel of leaves. Darkness surrounded them. The drums deadened.

"Where are we going?"

He squeezed her hand and kept walking, twigs popping in the mud.

16

He awoke in the morning with the breeze blowing across his face and a cold sheet pressed against his body. He turned his head into the wind. The girl lay beside him on the bed, watching.

"You were dreaming?"

He closed his eyes again. "I don't remember."

"You shouted."

"I don't remember my dreams."

He felt her gather the sheet up over her breasts.

"They say it's the dead trying to come back . . . making up thoughts in your mind."

"Who says that?" He opened his eyes.

"People like the *mambo*, Rain."

A gust of air shot into the room, bumping the matted blind against the window frame. Outside the bungalow, branches clawed the walls. Moonshot turned to the open window, curling her back against him. He rolled toward her and put his arm around her, kissing her neck. His shirt dropped off the edge of the bed onto the floor; the open door to the closet squeaked. Moonshot dropped onto her back.

"It's only the wind," he said.

"Roger. There's something I didn't tell you." She shut her eyes. "I was afraid."

"Afraid of what?"

"There was a hole in the wall, in your parents' room, the day they were missing."

"There wasn't any hole."

Her eyes opened. She stared at the ceiling. "The next day it was gone. A big one. Like a window. There was plaster on the floor and on the bed."

"A hole?"

"As big as a window."

"But what happened to it? Why didn't you tell me?"

"I was afraid."

He got out of bed and pulled on his pants. Moonshot put on her dress and ran behind him down the beach to his parents' bungalow. Sand whipped through the air. Palm fronds crackled in the trees. A layer of grit covered the front porch of the bungalow. They opened the door.

"Where?"

"In the center. Above the bed."

"Was there blood?"

"No. The lamp was on the floor, and the door wouldn't close."

"Then what? What'd you do?"

"I looked in the bathroom, and then I went to the church. When I came back the next day, it was like this."

Roger knelt on the bed and rubbed his hand over the wall. "It's been replastered and painted. You're sure it was here the first time?"

"Yes."

"That big?"

She sat down on the bed. "I was afraid. I didn't know what to do. I prayed for it to go away."

He sat next to her, propping his elbows on his knees and putting his palms together.

"It's something bad," she said, "isn't it?"

"A gunshot? Dynamite? I don't know. Some kind of an explosion."

The wind shrieked through the rafters, rattling the pictures against the wall. He heard his name in the distance.

"Señor Roger."

He went to the door and saw the fat man plodding through the sand toward the bungalow, holding his apron to his thighs with both hands.

"What is it, Pepe?"

"*Sargento* de León, señor. He wants to see you." Pepe brushed his hair back and pushed down a corner of his apron. "Now, señor. He's waiting like a bull without the balls."

"What?"

"No balls," shouted Pepe. "He's waiting like a bull after someone cuts off the balls." The fat man turned around and hiked away.

Roger left the girl at the door and stumbled onto the beach, shielding his eyes with an arm and cupping a hand over his nose. He crossed the beach to the back of the hotel. Sergeant de León lay stretched out in a chair in the blown-out office, his fingers laced behind his head, his feet propped on top of a box. Down his T-shirt twisted a gold chain with a silver crucifix clipped to the end. He shoveled a toothpick with his tongue from one corner of his mouth to the other and followed Roger with his eyes as he came up the back steps and into the room.

"Where is the money, *Americano?*"

"What money?"

The sergeant folded his brown arms across his chest. "The money from the safe."

"You have it."

"If I have the money, I will not be here. If I have the money, I will be enjoying the day some other place with beer and women and four walls without the wind. So you see, *Americano,* I do not have the money."

"You want a beer?" asked Roger.

The wind hummed through a patch of chicken wire in the wall. The sergeant uncrossed his arms and legs and stood up.

"It's your father's money, no?" He walked toward Roger.

"Yeah."

"And you think he should have it."

"Sure."

The sergeant planted a foot on the chair beside Roger,

flogging his dusty boot with a hand. "So you took the money."

"No. I didn't take it."

The sergeant's foot hit the floor. He put his hands on his hips and leaned forward, staring into Roger's face. "The money is missing, *Americano*."

"When?"

"Last night."

"It could've been anybody."

"It could've been anybody," mimicked the sergeant. Saliva dripped from his toothpick onto the floor. "We must be honest with each other."

Roger stared at the black eyes.

"*Bueno*." The sergeant arched his back and paced the room with his hands clasped behind him. "It's very funny. I see you at the Carnival and then I don't see you all night. You have a good time?"

"Yeah."

"And where were you?"

"In my room."

"Alone?"

"No."

"Ah. With a lady?"

"Maybe."

"And the money."

"No. Not the money. I didn't take the money."

The sergeant stopped and faced Roger. "It is a very serious mistake, señor."

"It's your mistake. I don't have the money. Anybody could've taken it. You could've taken it."

Sergeant de León removed the toothpick from his

mouth and aimed it at Roger's forehead. "Señor, for a man who spits on the eyeballs of the dead bodies rotting in the sun, life is cheap. It is good to remember who you are, no, *Americano?* And where you are. Isla Grande is very small. Like a tit on the water."

The sergeant sucked at the air and inserted the toothpick into his mouth. He walked to the edge of the building and jumped, the red dust exploding when he landed and blowing up into Roger's face.

"*Americano,*" he called. "This tit is only big enough for one pair of lips." He laughed and stomped away, swaggering against the wind.

Roger went into the vacant restaurant and sat down at the bar beside Gloria. She stirred an orange drink with a straw.

"Roger. I missed you last night. You have a good time?"

"Yeah."

"Me, too. We dance all the night and all the morning." She winked at Pepe. "Almost. And I almost got married, but the priest is drunk so we got married anyway. Not very legal, but it's okay for Carnival, no?"

"And where's the groom?" asked Pepe. He set a large glass of orange juice in front of Roger.

"He's gone. The shortest honeymoon I ever had. He even left without saying good-bye."

"Who's the lucky man?" asked Pepe.

"Señor Robinson."

"He left?" said Roger.

"Not even the good-bye kiss."

"Pepe, he left?"

"Sí, señor. An early bird catching the worms."

"He didn't say anything?"

The fat man polished the bar top with a towel. "Only he was leaving for business and he had a good time. But I don't believe him. He's a man who is always working."

"He wasn't working with me," said Gloria.

Pepe snickered and slapped at the counter with the towel.

"You're tired, Roger? It's still Carnival and I'm divorced now." She peeled off a paper ring from her finger and rolled it into a ball.

"You knew Smith before?"

"I don't want to talk about him."

"Gloria."

"You're jealous."

"I'm not jealous. Just tell me about him."

Gloria pinched her straw and sipped. "He's a nice man. He likes to spend money, and he speaks Spanish very good."

"What kind of person is he?"

Gloria dipped the straw up and down in her drink. "Strong and lots of energy. But I don't trust him."

"Why not?"

"He says things he doesn't mean."

"Like what?"

"Like, 'I love you.'"

Roger gazed out the window.

"See," said Gloria. "You're jealous."

"Do you know where he lives?"

"You want to go fight him?"

"Jesus Christ, Gloria. Where does he live?"

She looked at her drink and bobbed the straw. "He has an apartment in the city."

"You have the address?"

"No."

"Can you get it?"

"What for?"

"Is there a telephone here, Pepe?"

"No, señor. Only the radio . . . and it's not always working."

"Try to call by radio when you get the address. Okay, Gloria?"

"And what will you do for me?"

"Please."

"You are too cheap, Roger." She tossed the rolled-up paper ring on the counter. "Excuse me for the bathroom." She slipped off the bar stool and traipsed away, her hips swishing from side to side in her Carnival dress.

Pepe shook his head. "Hot stuff. No?"

Out the window, spray tore from the tops of the swells in the channel and slashed back at the sea. Waves exploded on the coral reef. The glass louvers in the dining room howled.

"Storm?"

"Only the wind," said Pepe. "A storm without the rain."

Roger nodded at Gloria's glass. "What's she drinking?"

"Tequila."

"Maybe she needs some more for the address."

Pepe unhooked a goblet from the rack above the bar and filled it with crushed ice, tequila, and orange juice. He dropped in two red cherries and a green straw.

Roger got up and walked to the door as Gloria's footsteps left the bathroom behind him.

"You are homo," she called. "Gay. Fruitcake. *Maricón.*"

He banged the door open with his shoulder and went outside onto the porch into the wind. The sea foamed. Floating through the air, particles of salt gleamed in the sunlight. Mist webbed his face. He closed his eyes and lifted up his chin. A patter rolled behind him across the roof of the building, pinging on the corrugated tin. He turned around and opened his eyes and saw the rain coming on him.

17

When the squall surged out into the channel, Roger wandered down the beach and around the peninsula to the town. Flower petals and bits of red and purple paper lay scattered on the shore. A bell rang. Men, women, and children in pressed white clothes walked up the steps of the white church. An organ trilled inside, voices sang, hands clapped. Roger crossed the street and climbed the stairs, past a man holding open the great door with his shoulder.

Inside, the congregation nodded their heads and flopped their handkerchiefs to the beat. A man in a black suit swung his arms up and down in front of a choir as the baritones faded at the end of a phrase and the sopranos lifted the last note on. Robed in black, a bible tucked under his arm, a priest stood beside the altar and smiled on the people. The fringe of his frock jiggled with the movement of his tapping shoe.

The music stopped in a crescendo and the room settled. The man in the black suit eased the choir into their pews, and the priest bowed to the cross and turned to the people. The last sounds of the organ echoed off the ceiling as the clergyman raised the black book in the air.

"'And he said unto me, My grace is sufficient for thee: for my strength is made perfect in weakness. Most gladly therefore will I rather glory in my infirmities, that the power of Christ may rest upon me.

"'Therefore I take pleasure in infirmities, in reproaches, in necessities, in persecutions, in distresses for Christ's sake: for when I am weak . . .'"

Roger left the church.

Down the steps he crossed the street to the beach and sat down in the sand. Swells tumbled through the channel, bringing houses in and out of view on the far shore. The sun shone in patches on the sea. A pair of white gulls floated toward the mainland.

"Are you angry?"

Moonshot knelt beside him and touched his shoulder.

He shook his head.

"I was afraid. I should have told you."

"It's okay. It doesn't matter. I just don't know what happened."

"You were inside the church?"

"The church doesn't make sense either. It looks Catholic. But the other day that lady was doing the chanting. And today the music and clapping. People don't clap and sing like that in a Catholic church."

"They don't?"

"No."

"What do they do?"

"They sit and pray."

"That's what we do."

"And you clap and sing gospels and chant."

Moonshot gazed out at the water and then stood up. "Come with me." She walked toward the street and stopped and waved at him. "Come."

He got up and followed her across the street and behind the great white church to the side of the mountain.

"Where?"

She lifted her dress to her knees and entered the bushes, and he followed behind her. Lizards slithered before his feet. He swatted a spider web off his face and climbed past a banana stalk lying in the mud with fruit flies hovering in swarms around the broken skins. In the distance an animal shrieked. Roger slipped and clipped a piece of fungus off a log with his hand and pulled himself up the mountain.

Near the top a path developed along a ridge and led to a shack under a monkeypod tree. Roosters scampered over the swollen roots and fallen crimson stamens. Moonshot waited on a bluff overlooking the great white church and the pier.

"The house of the *mambo*," she said. "Rain. The one we saw in the church. Maybe she can help with your parents."

"She finds missing people?"

In the doorway of the shack stood a woman in a long red gown, a strand of colored beads across her chest. She motioned to Roger and Moonshot with her hand, and they went inside where the mud changed to dirt and a candle glowed in a far corner of the room. Against a wall a fire smoldered in a pit, the smoke twisting up and escaping through a hole in the roof.

The old woman dipped her fingers into a bowl of water on a table and scrubbed them. A chartreuse scarf fluttered on a nail above the window behind her.

"This is Mr. Roger," said Moonshot. "His parents own the hotel—the people who are missing."

The old woman massaged her knuckles in the basin.

"Mr. Roger would like to learn something about them, where they are, what happened to them."

Rain sat down in a rocking chair, curling her hands over the wooden arms as water dripped from her fingers. She stared at Roger. "Does he believe?" The rocking chair creaked.

"He wants to," said Moonshot.

The old woman stood up and walked to the fire, stirring the coals with a stick and placing her hands in the smoke. "Then bring him to the meeting tonight."

"Thank you," said Moonshot. She whispered to Roger, "Do you have anything for her?"

He wrinkled his forehead.

"Money," she whispered.

He took out some bills from his pocket and gave her one, and she put it on the table on their way out.

She led him along the ridge and up the mountain until they came to a lighthouse mounted on a knoll.

Gulls soared mute over the channel. He grabbed her arm and stopped her.

"What meeting?"

"A séance. Have you ever been to one?"

"You're kidding."

"She's spoken with many people in the other world."

Moonshot opened the metal door of the lighthouse, and they entered, clanking up the spiral staircase. From the platform at the top, they walked outside onto the deck, their clothes beating against their bodies in the wind. Whitecaps puffed up on the sea and faded away, and new caps rose and died in the troughs.

Moonshot inhaled. "It blows so hard up here . . . like it's trying to smother you."

He bowed his head into the wind.

At the rail, she guided him around to the other side of the tower and pointed at the mainland. "You can see the cars on the road. See the trails?"

He leaned against the tower and watched the streams of dust rise up and disappear, the iron lighthouse trembling on his spine in the wind.

18

The motor whined in the darkness. Roger spun the skiff away from the hotel pier and headed out into the cove, through the mist, and around the reef. Fires sparkled in the mountains on the mainland. The boat plowed over the waves in the channel and stuttered down the middle of the strait. In front of the town, he slowed the skiff and stopped the engine, slipping the oars into their locks and rowing.

Canoes and dinghies bobbed near the shore; wind waves lapped against the hulls. Electric floodlights on the church beamed into the air above the belfry. A few dark figures roamed the dirt road. Roger rowed to the stern of a powerboat anchored in front of the town and tied the painter around a stanchion. He climbed aboard the listing vessel.

Moonlight reflected its sheen off the cabin windows.

Roger's shoes screaked across the wet deck. He forced the door to the main cabin, banging on it with his shoulder until the wood splintered and the door jerked open. High in the moonlight on both sides of the room, stacks of wooden crates reached to the ceiling. He went inside.

He took a knife out of a drawer in the galley and wedged the blade into the corner of a box, prying up a board and peeling it away with his fingers. Metal gleamed through a mound of shredded paper. He reached in and touched the barrel of a gun. Oil trickled into his palm. He re-covered the crate, hammering the lid shut with the butt of the knife, and stood for a moment in the center of the cabin among the boxes. Wiping the oil off on his pants, he went outside and got into the skiff, dropping the line and pushing away from the boat with the blade of an oar.

At the beach Roger fumbled the paddles into the bottom of the skiff and dragged the boat across the sand to a palm tree. Moonshot stood beside the porch of a nearby house. They met and walked up the steps to an open doorway with a curtain of seashells crackling in the breeze. Voices sang inside the darkened building.

"Did you bring the pictures?"

He took out a photograph of his mother and father from his shirt pocket and handed it to her.

Inside, at a table full of pictures and burning incense, Moonshot lit two candles and propped the photograph between them. Women at the head of the room held out feathered charms and dolls and painted crosses as they swayed to the rhythm of their monotone voices. Mopping at arms and shoulders and trance-covered faces, young girls clutching towels crawled among the scores of kneeling men and women. Roger and Moonshot sat down against the back wall.

Swirling with the women in the front of the room danced Rain, her body jerking and convulsing. She hugged a picture against the sweat-darkened bodice of her dress. The chanters droned. The curtain of shells clacked in the doorway. Rain staggered to the first row of people and collapsed, and a young girl scrambled across the floor on her hands and knees and wiped the old woman's neck and fanned her forehead.

Roger and Moonshot stepped through the crowd and sat down beside the glassy-eyed *mambo* as she swung her body from side to side, mumbling.

"Baron Samedi," said Moonshot.

Perspiration dripped off the old woman's face and onto the picture she pressed to her bosom.

"Baron Samedi, we're looking for two people. Can you tell us something about them?"

The attendant reached up and sponged Rain's brow. The old woman directed her gaze at Roger's chest and huffed.

"Mr. Ben Lord and Mrs. Birdie. Can you tell us about them? Do you know where they are?"

The *mambo's* eyes widened. Her lips bulged forward. "Dead."

"They're dead?" said Moonshot.

"But . . . he . . . is . . . still . . . here."

The young girl blotted Rain's cheeks and chin and

stared at Roger.

"Ben . . . Lord . . . is . . . here."

"How can he be here if he's dead?" said Roger.

"Here," said Rain, pointing a finger at Roger and gaping at his chest. "In . . . the . . . body . . . of . . . the . . . son."

The old woman fell back into the girl's arms, and the attendant cradled her head in her lap, covering the neck with a towel, massaging the shoulders, watching Roger.

He got up and strode out of the house. Moonshot followed him outside to the porch.

"She's crazy," he said.

"Why?"

"You believe her? My father's come back from the dead? In my body? Christ." He went down the steps and stopped and turned around. "Spirits? Who the hell's Baron Samedi?"

"The saint of graveyard crosses."

"Bullshit."

He walked away from the house, kicking sand, and she ran behind him. He stopped and turned to her again.

"If you need to believe in all this crap so you can feel good, then fine. But don't put it off on me. You believe it? You can have it. If it makes you feel good, then great. But don't expect me to go around lighting candles or believing old women who put on shows so they can be important or get money or I don't know what. You believe that crap?"

She looked at him.

"Well?" He crouched down and sat in the sand.

"You don't have to believe it."

"I just don't understand it." He grabbed a handful of sand and heaved it at the water. "I went to my father's boat tonight."

He shoveled up another handful of sand and squeezed it.

"You know what I found?"

She watched him.

"Guns. Goddamned boxes of machine guns." He threw the sand down the beach.

"On your father's boat?"

"The powerboat. The goddamned powerboat. I don't understand it. What's he got guns for?"

"I was trying to help."

Roger flattened a mound of sand with his fist.

"Maybe you can't understand it," she said.

He looked at the fires on the mainland.

"Maybe the reasons all disappeared."

"Yeah. Maybe nothing here makes any sense. Maybe it just happens. Maybe it's not even supposed to make sense."

He went to the palm tree and untied the skiff and hauled it through the sand and into the water, racing the engine and rushing out past the flush of the island to the middle of the channel where he cut the motor and lay down in the bottom of the boat and drifted, rain falling on his face in the moonlight.

19

They plodded through the slanted rays of the afternoon sun with their feet squishing in the mud. The town appeared through the trees, and the two men slapped at the last pieces of jungle and stamped onto the dusty road, kicking the clay off their shoes.

"What do you think he wants?" said Roger.

"Only he wants to speak with the son of Señor Ben. He is not a man for talking, señor. They say he killed his mother for the gold in her teeth."

"His mother?"

Pepe slashed an index finger across his throat.

They walked along the row of colored houses to the pier, where the black Colombian schooner waited alongside. Six bare-chested sailors sprawled under an awning on the foredeck, throwing down cards and cursing. Unlit cigarettes drooped from their mouths. Knife handles stuck up from the waistbands of their pants.

Pepe spoke to a boy braiding rope on top of the cabin. The card players turned around as the boy answered, and Roger and Pepe climbed aboard and went below. Barrels of diesel fuel jammed the cabin. Two men with quarts of beer at their elbows sat at a table, counting money. Pepe looked at Roger and nodded at a chair, and they sat down.

One of the men picked up a knife and pinned a stack of bills to the table. He grabbed his bottle and guzzled, his greasy forehead shining in the light from the hatch. The other man stared into Roger's eyes. Diamond earrings glinted in his earlobes; a fly crawled across his bald head.

The man with the greasy forehead put down his bottle and spoke in Spanish, slurring his words.

"He wants to know if there's anything you want to buy," said Pepe.

The two Colombians watched Roger.

"Who is he?"

"His name is Salvador. But we should call him Señor."

"He doesn't speak English?"

"I don't think so. He's speaking Spanish now."

"Ask him what he has to sell."

The bald man lifted up his bottle and probed the end of it with his tongue. Pus oozed out of a scab on his forearm. Pepe spoke to the greasy man and turned to Roger.

"He says, 'Many things.'"

"What do you usually get from him?"

"Nothing. I trade with the sailors on the pier, not with the *capitán*."

"Then what's he asking us for?"

"I don't know, señor." Pepe smiled at the two men.

"Tell him we don't want anything."

The man with the black fly on his head lifted his chin at Roger and asked a question.

"What was that?"

"He wants to know if you're the real son of Señor Ben."

"Does he know my father?"

"It's possible, señor."

Salvador drooped his hand over a pile of money and spoke, pointing to a gold tooth in his mouth.

"He says if you want to buy something, he will make you a good price. He says he likes gold very much."

Salvador and the bald man laughed.

"What's he want me to buy?"

"It's not a good idea to ask so many questions. It's better to answer only Sí or No."

"Then tell him No."

The two sailors horsed down the rest of their beer. Salvador lowered his bottle and grunted, brushing the back of his hand across the table.

"Time to go now, señor," said Pepe.

"Ask him if he's done business with my father before."

The fat man looked at the Colombians. "It's not the best thing to do."

"Ask him, Pepe."

Salvador tossed his bottle at an open porthole, shat-

tering the neck on the edge of the window and scattering glass on the floor. He yanked the knife out of
the table.

"Time to go," said Pepe. He got up and Roger followed him outside.

On the way back through the jungle, the sun set,
coloring the sky orange behind the foliage. From the
hotel Roger walked to the end of the pier and sat
down. Water gurgled at the pilings as swells surged up
onto the shore. Footsteps pounded on the pier, bending the wooden planks under Roger's hands. A figure
ambled forward. On the mountain ridge overhead the
lighthouse beacon flashed.

"Do you enjoy the night?" called Sergeant de León.
His boots stopped at Roger's fingertips. He gazed at
the cove.

"Yeah."

The sergeant tucked his hands inside the front of his
fatigues. Tied around his neck, a plastic poncho hung
over his shoulders. He took a breath and exhaled.

"The salt air. Perfect for the health, no? You enjoy
good health, señor?"

"What do you want?"

Sergeant de León squatted, a wet toothpick between his lips. "The money."

"I don't have it."

"I do not like you, señor."

"And I don't like you."

"Then, *Americano,* we must put our differences
aside."

The sergeant stood up and looked out at the sea

again. He put his hands on his hips and arched his back.

"It's like death tonight, no? Cold on the bones. Strange how everything changes so fast. One day it's warm and the air is sweet like the mango. And then something happens and everything is cold. The wind blows and blows. They say it's the air that comes from the north. The summer is gone and the winter is here. All at once the good things go away. Sometimes it's the same with people, no, *Americano*?"

"You know what happened to my parents?"

"I am only talking about the weather, señor. But, perhaps, if you can find the money, I can find some information to help you."

"I don't have the money. But I have an idea who does."

The toothpick squirmed to the other side of the sergeant's mouth.

"And who is this person, señor?"

"Robinson Smith. He left in the morning, the day after the money was taken."

"I am noticing this, too." The sergeant paused and removed his toothpick and put the other end of it in his mouth. "I hope, señor, that you are right."

"What do you know about my parents?"

The sergeant stared into the darkness. "The day they disappeared I came to see your father. He owes me some money from playing poker. Not very much, but a little. The hotel is empty so I go to their room and I see the door is open. And inside there is the wall with a hole."

"You saw it?"

"It was not a good thing for me. He owes me the money and I go to the room and I have to say he is not there, and the room looks very bad. The *coronel* will come from the city and maybe I will lose my job because of the trouble."

"You covered it up?"

"I cover up the hole and I look for the person who did this thing, but I don't find him yet."

"Was it a gunshot?"

"I don't know, señor, but I think so."

"Who did it?"

"This I do not know. Perhaps this man Robinson Smith has an idea. He has the money, no?"

"You think they're dead?"

"I am doing my best," said the sergeant. "When I find the answer, I will tell you."

Sergeant de León walked down the pier, scuffing his heels across the wood.

The scraping halted. "*Americano,*" called the sergeant. "You know the girl, Moonshot?"

Roger watched the dark figure hovering at the end of the pier. The poncho rustled in the breeze.

"You know she is married, señor?" Sergeant de León's toothpick glistened. "To me." The boots swished into the sand, and the silhouette raised its arm. "Have a good night, señor."

20

Dawn brightened the horizon, unveiling a body of gray water and a white line of surf rolling on the reef. Roger sat on the front porch of his bungalow, listening to the sound of an engine in the distance. A dory with boxes piled to the shoulders of two men riding fore and aft chugged around the end of the peninsula and into the cove. The boat docked at the hotel pier and the men unloaded a box, lugging it between them around the far side of the building, then hurrying back to the pier.

Roger jogged down the steps of the bungalow and along the gravel path to the back of the hotel. In the shadow of the building, under a clump of twisted palm trees, a crate with the word EXPLOSIVOS stenciled on its lid sat cocked against a wooden shed.

Footsteps hissed in the sand alongside the hotel.

Robinson Smith and a man with a gun tucked in the front of his pants staggered sideways, hauling another crate. They glanced at Roger, set the box down on the ground, and leaned it against the shed.

"What's this?"

Robinson Smith reached into his shirt pocket and pulled out a pack of cigarettes and a matchbook. "Dynamite." He took out a cigarette and hung it between his lips while he tore out a match. "For blowing up a reef."

Roger nodded at the other man. "Who's he?"

"Diver."

The man slumped against the boxes and folded his arms, the index finger on his right hand lopped off at the first knuckle.

"Aren't you waiting for my father?"

Robinson Smith tossed the match away and blew smoke out the side of his mouth. "Weather's kind of freaky. I don't think he'd want me to wait."

"You're taking the powerboat?"

He nodded and spoke to the diver in Spanish. The man straightened up and went toward the pier.

"You know de León's looking for you?" said Roger.

Robinson Smith dragged on his cigarette.

"My father's money's gone."

"The son of a bitch probably still has it." Robinson Smith exhaled out his nose as the cigarette hung in his mouth. "Tell him to go screw himself." He strode toward the pier.

The two men hoisted another crate out of the dory, and Roger ran behind the hotel and down the gravel path. At the garden next to the last bungalows, Moon-shot knelt in the dirt, digging. He slowed and walked up behind her.

"There's no money."

She turned around.

"You can't do that," he said. "There's no money."

She stood up among the flowers, holding a weed in her hand.

"There's nothing to pay you with."

She brushed her empty hand on her dress. Scarlet orchids blanketed her feet. "They'll die."

"Why didn't you tell me you're married?" he said.

"I'm not."

"De León told me."

"I'm not married."

"He says so. You live with him?"

"We're not married," she said. "He's never there. He never gives us anything. Just some food."

"You have children?"

"Sisters and brothers."

"You wanted money from me? That's how you get your money?"

She stared at him.

"You don't care what you do? Why don't you work?"

"There is no work. Even the ones who have a job everyday don't have enough money."

"Why?"

"It's not enough."

"Why don't you go to school? Send your brothers to learn something."

"There's no school without money."

"Then get help from someone."

"From who? No one can help us. We're all the same. If your sisters and brothers were crying because there wasn't any food, what would you do?"

"I don't know."

"You'd do something. If you were a woman, you'd do anything with anyone to keep your family from suffering. And you'd feel lucky to have a way. If you lived like this, Roger, what would you do?"

He turned and ran down the path and off between the palm trees to the beach, picking up chunks of white coral from the sand and hurling them at the water. Roosters shrieked from the mangroves, and he spun around and slung a stone into the bushes. The roosters screeched louder. He whirled toward the sailboats and shouted out Dutch's name, his voice echoing back to him across the water, screaming.

21

The jeep bumped along the road, slapping through nets of hanging vines. Dewdrops exploded across the windshield and splattered Roger's elbow. Through the trees and across the road seeped ripples of gray mist. Dutch rested his bottle between his legs and leaned forward, switching on the windshield wipers.

"Dumb idea," he said. "Real dumb."

"They're taking the guns," said Roger.

"So what? You're going to arrest them?"

The road zig-zagged through the bushes. They passed a truck loaded with palm branches, wallowing up a hill with a flat tire. Clearings in the jungle flashed by, shacks standing in the shade, women scrubbing clothes, white chickens pecking at the mud.

The mist lifted, and purple rings circled the drops of water on the windshield. At a point overlooking the sea, Dutch pulled off to the side. Roger looked through a pair of binoculars at the white powerboat plowing along the coast.

"Think he's going to the canal?"

"Too damn far."

Dutch took a swig from his bottle, and they drove down the hill past a collection of boarded-up shelters and surged across a gorge and up another hill to a cliff above a bay. They pulled over again. A river with boulders humped on its banks cut through a valley and into the sea. A stone wall encircled the town. Cannon sat perched on a bluff.

"He's coming in," said Roger. "What is this place?"

"Portobello. Where the Spanish brought all the gold and sent it to Spain."

Roger squinted through the glasses. "A fort?"

The bony man put the bottle to his lips and looked in the rear view mirror. "Someone's following us."

Roger turned around. "Drive down a little and see who it is."

"Then what?" Dutch took another swallow.

The white boat powered to the end of the bay and swept around in front of a sea wall.

"Someone's coming out in a boat," said Roger. "They've got the boxes out on deck." He lowered the glasses. "Let's go."

"You wanted to see where he's going. Now you know."

"But maybe they're going someplace else. Maybe they'll put the stuff in a car and drive somewhere."

"So what?"

"All right. I'll walk." He opened the door.

The jeep lurched forward. "You dumb ass," shouted Dutch. "Get in."

At the bottom of the hill, the road ran through a graveyard with tilted headstones. The jeep crossed a wooden bridge and thrummed onto a cobblestone street. Between two rows of moss-covered buildings, a skiff drifted toward the white powerboat. Four men hauled boxes across the beach and into an alley.

"They still behind us?"

Dutch looked up at the mirror.

"Drop me off up here," said Roger.

"What for?"

"Drop me off."

The jeep turned a corner, and Roger opened the door and jumped, rolling in the street and scrambling into an alley. He pressed his back against a brick wall as the second car sped past. A trickle of blood wet his arm. Out of a window slipped a cat, eyeing the ground where a swarm of flies buzzed over the carcass of a rat. Roger crept down the passage toward the water.

Halfway along the alley a yellow light shone above a door. Roger cupped his hands over a windowpane, chunks of broken glass crackling under his feet. The window opened. The barrel end of a revolver jarred against his forehead. A man grabbed his collar and dragged him across the windowsill and into the room, throwing him onto the floor and pressing the gun against his temple.

A light bulb swung from a cord on the ceiling. Urine smelled in the dirt. The man yanked him to his feet and pushed him into a chair, clubbing him across the skull with the gun. Roger clutched his head and slumped forward, blood dripping through his fingers.

Outside, footsteps shuffled down the alleyway. The diver and another man entered the room, struggling with a crate. They looked at Roger and stopped. The diver set his end of the box down and shouted at the other two men as he ran out of the room. The two unhooked a rope from the wall and tied Roger's hands behind his back and lashed his feet to the legs of the chair.

More footsteps rushed through the alley and the door opened. The diver marched in, followed by Dutch, carrying his bottle. He closed the door.

The diver crouched on a box in the corner of the room as Dutch yelled at the other two men in Spanish and swung a chair out from the table, straddling it and gulping from his bottle.

"You okay?"

Blood trickled down Roger's cheek. "What is it, Dutch? What's going on?"

The three men on the boxes watched the Americans.

"It's better not to know. Believe me."

"You knew about this and you never said anything?"

"There's nothing to say."

"What happened to my father?"

"I don't know."

"Were they smuggling guns and cocaine?"

"I can't tell you."

"Why not?"

Dutch stood up and guzzled from his bottle. He

walked to the door and wiped his mouth.

"They're my parents."

"Do you know," said Dutch, "that these guys want to kill you?"

The three men stared at Roger.

"You've got two choices. Get on a plane and go back to the States and forget everything. Or stay here in a place you don't understand, where you don't belong, and end up getting shot or kidnapped and never heard of again."

"Like my parents?"

"Right. Like your goddamned parents. You don't understand, do you? I don't know what happened to them. I don't know. And I don't want to know."

"Then just tell me what you do know."

"Then we'd both disappear."

"Who was following us?"

"That son of a bitch, de León."

"Why?"

"I don't know."

Dutch walked into the shadows and back out into the light in the center of the room. He sat down in front of Roger. "Forget it."

"I don't know where they are. I don't know if they're alive or dead. I don't know anything. I just want to know."

Dutch turned around and spoke to the three men. The diver shouted, waving his arms and pointing at the boxes on the floor. Dutch stood up and kicked over the chair. He walked to the door, where he took another swallow.

"I don't know what's going to happen to you, kid. But you want an answer, maybe you'll get it."

He left, followed by the diver with the half finger.

The other two men drew knives out of their boots and ripped a strip of cloth from Roger's shirt and wrapped it around his eyes, cinching the knot at the base of his skull. They sliced off the ropes at his ankles and jerked him to his feet, pulling him to the doorway and wrenching his elbows back. He banged his foot on the threshold and stumbled out the door and into the stink of the alley.

22

The throbbing at the back of Roger's skull weakened and the blindfold fell away, brushing across his face. He squinted at the sunlight. The two men from the room sucked at canteens. Army packs and automatic rifles hung over their shoulders.

Snot dribbled out the nose of one of the men as he shoved his canteen into Roger's mouth. Water gushed down Roger's chin and onto his shirt. He gagged and backed away. The men jeered at him and jabbed their rifles into his kidneys, pushing him down the trail. They resealed their canteens and marched ahead, laughing.

The column of three hiked into a forest and climbed along a ridge covered in shade. Pieces of bark cracked under their feet; birds trilled in the bush. Perspiration blackened Roger's shirt. He wiped his chin on his shoulder and blinked the sweat away from his eyes. The path dipped down into a valley, and the vegetation grew greener. The smell of fern leaves and mint filled the air. A whistle piped. One of the men raised his rifle and shot into the trees. A bird with red tail feathers tore through the branches and plopped on the ground.

"*Uno,*" said the man.

The other man shot at the opposite side. A red ball fell in the leaves. "*Uno,*" he said.

The first man aimed his rifle at Roger, and Roger turned and ducked into the bushes. "*Bang,*" yelled the man. "*Dos.*"

The two men cackled and lowered their guns against their bodies and trudged ahead.

Late in the afternoon they trod up a side path to a wooden house hidden in the jungle. Smoke streamed out of a hole in the rusted roof. One of the men whacked a boot on the foundation of the building, and an old woman appeared in the shadows of the porch. A teenage girl peered around her shoulder. The man asked a question and the old woman shook her head. He shouted at her and pointed his rifle at Roger, and they butted him up the steps, past the girl and the jabbering old woman and into the house.

Up between the floorboards and through the knotholes and cracks in the walls, sunlight slanted into the shack. Cobwebs drooped from the tin roof. A wall of gray snapshots faced the only window in the room, where a fly buzzed in and out and a saucer of salt lay on the sill. Below the window stood a table and three chairs.

The two men pushed Roger into one of the chairs and cut off his bindings while the girl and the old woman walked past them into another room. The old woman chirped among the clanging of pots and pans, and one of the men went to the doorway and spoke, the old woman's voice wrangling over his. The girl entered with a handful of spoons and forks and arranged them on the table. The man with the dripping nose slipped his rifle over his shoulder and stood by the table, staring at the young girl's breasts.

She left the room and came back with three glasses and placed them beside the spoons. The man sniffled against his shirt and picked up Roger's fork and moved over to the girl, whispering to her and stroking the side of her face with his knuckles. She gazed down at the floor. He pressed the fork into her chin and lifted up the back of her dress and massaged her buttocks. He cooed, leaning close to her face, and she broke away from him and ran out of the room. He pointed the fork after her and sneered.

After they ate, they took Roger outside to a tree behind the kitchen, where in a puddle of water he washed the dried blood off his face and arms and urinated. They brought him back into a small room with a cot and strapped his wrists and ankles to the bedposts and went out, shutting the door and flipping a metal hasp. A lock snapped. Moonlight flowed into the room through an open window, framing a wooden crucifix on the wall.

A patter drummed across the tin roof of the room and dropped onto a chest below the window. A tingle

ran down Roger's leg. He stiffened. Another patter
dashed over the metal, jumped to the chest, flopped
onto the bed. His leg prickled as the roof thundered.

Outside the room a cat shrieked, and a flurry of
scratches scuttled back down the hallway, under the
door, up onto the bed, and over his thigh. The wooden
chest rattled beside him. A loud thump hit the wall.
The pricking swarmed over his body as little feet leaped
onto his legs and stomach. He forced the side of his
face into the mattress and shut his eyes until the screeching and clawing stopped. In the silence, he turned his
head to the window. From the top of the wooden chest
to the floor, blood dripped off the tail of a dead rat in
the moonlight.

Early the next morning they left, a mantle of steam
covering the jungle, clinging to the trees. Moisture
spiraled down the vines and splashed in the mud. Mos-
quitoes bit Roger's ears. Behind him slogged the two
men, spraying bursts of gunfire into the bushes and
mocking the paths of the falling birds with their hands.

Over a hill and through a valley, they came to a
village of tiled roofs beside a stream. Plots of land
tiered the mountainside. Children's voices echoed along
the river. Riding a donkey up the path, an old man
dozed, his head nodding with the clomp of the animal's
hoofs.

The two men left their guns in a shack bordering the
jungle and cut the ropes off of Roger's hands. Gripping his elbows, they led him along a street of shuttered buildings, stopping at a corner house with a red
bougainvillea twining up the front wall and hooking in

the air. One of the men rapped on the door. Inside the house a slow melody lilted from a piano. The front door opened.

A maid ushered Roger through a mirrored foyer and into a living room. He sat down on a velvet sofa framed with vases of sunflowers and red roses on the end tables. Potted plants rested below a window. A water-color of lush mountains hung on the wall in front of him. The piano tinkled. Heeltaps clicked across the tiled floor, and a man in a dark sports coat and pants entered, his shirt opened at the collar, a white carna-tion in the coat lapel.

"You're Ben's son?"

Roger nodded and stood up.

"My name is Fernando de la Cruz." He shook Roger's hand. "You're hungry? Something to drink?"

Roger tucked in his torn shirt and sat down.

The man sank into a leather armchair and folded a leg over a knee. A gold watch gleamed on his wrist. "I'm sorry to hear about your father and mother. We were good friends."

"You know what happened to them?"

The man fit his palms over the armrests of the chair. "I'm sorry I can't tell you. I don't know myself. But I'm afraid of the worst."

"What's that mean?"

"There are no easy answers."

"What was my father doing with the guns?"

The man brushed a piece of lint off his trousers. "Helping us."

"Helping who?"

"You haven't been in Panama very long?"

"Maybe two weeks."

Fernando de la Cruz put his hands in his lap. "Most Americans think we're all the same. We're small countries and we speak the same language. But here the similarities end.

"Each of us has our own history and our own problems. Problems with the land, with education, with the economy. No one understands this. And then, we're not Americans. We don't have the right to protest." He picked a loose thread from his pants leg and dropped it on the floor.

"I have lived in your country for eighteen years. I was a professor at one of your best universities. My wife is American and all of my children were born in your country. But this is my home. All the land you walked on today, and most of the land you walked on yesterday, once belonged to my grandfather. For many years now, the government—the military—has denied my country the right to choose its own future. They arm themselves with weapons and money from the United States. The generals get rich and retire in Florida, and the people live as they have always lived.

"What are they afraid of? Who will attack us? Our borders are safe. The United States protects the canal. They're arming themselves against their own people. But we don't want a war. We want only the right to choose our own future."

The music stopped. A swinging door wobbled on its hinges. A blond woman walked around a corner, and the two men rose.

"My wife," said Fernando de la Cruz. "Catherine."

The woman offered her hand to Roger. "I'm sorry," she smiled. "You must forgive him. When he talks about politics, he doesn't know when to stop."

She smiled again and they sat down.

"I was telling him about our country. He's Ben's son."

"Your parents are wonderful people," she said.

"Your senators and congressmen," said Fernando, "they don't know what's happening down here. A few of them take a trip to Panama City, a fact-finding mission. They go to the canal. They have a reception or two. They don't see the people, the real people. They see the Hilton Hotel. They listen to the generals and to the ambassador. For them, we are too small, and there's the canal to think about. So they keep the dictator and the generals happy and ignore the rest. It is, after all, in the best interests of your government to keep the present government in control, even if it is a bad one."

A bell chimed and the maid came in and answered the front door. A woman was sobbing. The maid spoke to Fernando and he excused himself and went to the door.

"He's a psychologist," said his wife, rubbing a hand on the velvet. "Not a revolutionary. But he loves his country very much. If I made him choose, I think he would take it over anything." She smiled. "Even me."

The door closed and the psychologist crossed the room to his leather chair.

"You see," he said. "The most common problem I have. The woman's husband is out drinking. Every time he comes home drunk, he beats her. They have no money and four small children. I told her to bring him to see me when he's sober, and I'd talk to him. That's all I can do. There's no welfare here. No job training. No jobs. So he drinks up what little money they have and beats her to show he's still a man and to let out his anger. You see what we have to work against."

"And my father?"

"Your father and mother were friends of mine when I lived in the United States, before you were born. At first, we argued over everything, especially the politics of your country. In the end, we understood each other, and I think we both changed a little, he, a little more liberal, and I, a little more conservative. Some years ago, when your father retired from the army, they came to this house and visited me. I showed them my country and my people, and they bought a small hotel in the San Blas Islands. The hotel had problems, but they were able to take over the one on Isla Grande.

"Over the last few years the political situation has gotten much worse. There's no sign of improvement. We've had no choice but to arm ourselves. Your father's been able to help us as a link with the arms coming out of Colombia."

"Why? Why would he do something like that? He was a drillmaster."

Fernando de la Cruz straightened the crease in his pants.

"It might be hard to understand, but I think if he were here, he'd say it's for the people of my country. Something for them to use as a lever. Suppression is like a huge stone. You can see it in the way the people walk, in the way they drink and accept their suffering.

"One day I'll publish what I'm writing, the truth about our government, and then I'll send my wife and my children to the United States and begin to fight for what is ours. It's not the land or the money. If these things belong to anyone, they belong to God. What we're fighting for is dignity. As we are now, we have little more than the rights of animals. I think this is what your father saw, and what he learned to hate as much as I do."

"But my father would never fight here, even if he agreed with you."

"Perhaps he wouldn't fight another person's battle. But if he saw a fight that wasn't fair, he'd help to balance the sides. That's what he's done for us."

"And the cocaine?"

Fernando de la Cruz tilted his head.

"On my father's boat."

"I don't know anything about cocaine. I'd have nothing to do with it. I'm sure your father wouldn't either."

"What about the money in the safe at the hotel?"

"It's ours. It's used to buy the weapons. One of our men would bring it to him."

"Then Robinson Smith took the money from the *guardia*?"

"Yes."

"And Dutch works for you."

"Dutch used to make the deliveries from Isla Grande, but when your father left the San Blas, he was able to take over for him."

"It's a little hard to believe."

"Sometimes people live all their lives one way and then, in the end, find out that what they've been doing isn't what they really wanted. Other things suddenly mean more to them. Something they see or maybe something that happens to them changes them. They decide not to waste any more time doing what everyone else expects them to do. Age, in a way, can give freedom. It might be like this for your father."

"What happened to them?"

"There are many dangers in this country and many things done that no one sees. I'm sure that if it's possible, they'll return. I wish I could say more."

Roger looked at the woman and then back at Fernando. "I'm not sure I understand it all."

"I trust you not to repeat anything you've seen or heard today. And I ask one more thing." He clasped his hands together and sat on the edge of his chair. "When you return to the United States, tell the people about what you've seen. Not what I say or what someone else says about my country, but what you have seen. I believe that if the American people really knew what it was like here, what our people think and feel, then they wouldn't let what's happening here continue."

Roger nodded.

"The men who brought you will take you to a place where you can get a bus. From there you'll be able to get back to Isla Grande by tonight."

They stood up and shook hands. Catherine squeezed his arm and kissed him on the cheek. "Give our love to your parents," she said.

He nodded again.

Outside the house the two guerrillas sat slouched against the wall, sharing a bottle under the bougainvillea. A barefoot boy polished one of the men's boots. Other boys with shoeshine boxes stood around, watching the men drink as the red petals on the bougainvillea bobbed above them in the wind. Inside the house a minuet began to play, and the boys saw Roger and started toward him, wagging their rags in their hands and pointing at his tennis shoes.

23

The bus stopped at the shacks in front of the island and Roger got off. The truck skidded away in the dust. He walked toward the old man's shack, where a lantern glowed through the back window and accordions wheezed on a radio. Around the corner the dark boy pirouetted in the twilight, arms twisting in the air, eyes closed. A young girl slipped off the bench and went inside the house. The music softened, and the boy stumbled and opened his eyes. The boy's father stood in the doorway, gnawing on a hunk of dried beef.

"*Buenos noches*," said Roger.

The light from the house sparkled on the old man's beard as he chewed and nodded.

"Isla Grande?" Roger pointed to the channel.

The old man tore at the stick with his teeth. "*No hay sol.*"

"No sun," said the dark boy.

"Tell him I'll pay two dollars."

The old man shook his head.

Roger looked at the lights on the island. "Four."

The old man wagged a finger and stuffed the rest of the beef in his mouth. He turned and walked into the house.

Roger looked at the boy. "Will you take me?"

The young boy pulled up his shorts with one hand, the fly bowed open, the zipper torn away from its seam. "Five."

"Five dollars?"

The dark boy raised five fingers.

"Okay. Five."

At the beach they dragged the canoe across the sand and into the water as the boy jumped in.

"Why won't he take me?"

"Afraid," said the boy.

"Afraid of what?"

"*Los espíritus.*" The boy lifted his arms and flapped them.

"Birds?"

"Spirits. On the water."

"He's seen them?"

The dark boy nodded several times.

"And you're not afraid?"

"I look for their paddles in the moonlight."

"You've seen them, too?"

He started the engine. "I am so fast."

Roger got in and the boat slid across the slack water and into the channel, the first swells rolling the canoe

from side to side. The boat dipped and slugged into a
wave as pellets of water sprayed Roger's face. He
grabbed the edge of the seat and arched his back. The
angle steepened. The boat dropped into a trough, jar-
ring against another wave. Saltwater drenched the
inside of the boat, and they surged up the next crest.
Roger watched the lights on the island rise up out of
the black and fall and rise again and fall.

At the entrance to the cove, the sea flattened. Foam
floated on the reef. The boy slowed the engine and
guided the canoe toward the hotel and up alongside
the pier. Roger handed him five dollars and got out,
and the boy careened the boat in a J and sped back
toward the reef. Roger dropped down on his knees and
vomited into the water.

"Se . . . ñor Ro . . . ger."

Roger straightened his back as Pepe plodded down
the pier, waving both arms.

"Señor Roger." He stopped and pushed a ring into
Roger's hand. "They found the ring, señor." He pointed
to a fire on the beach. "You're okay?"

Roger stared at the ring. "Who?"

"A man on the beach. It's the ring of Mrs. Birdie,
no?"

Roger stumbled off the pier and down the beach to
the end of the cove, where a crowd of islanders stood
around a fire near the water. He pushed his way through
the onlookers to a man hunched over on the shore,
honing a knife against a stone. Blood coated the man's
arms, a string of intestines glistened beside the body of
a shark.

Roger held the ring out in front of the man's face. "You find this?"

The man looked up and nodded.

"Where?"

He pointed with his knife at the shark.

Roger's foot cracked across the man's chest, tumbling the knife in the sand. The man clutched his ribs, and Roger kicked him in the face, rolling him over the intestines as blood gushed from the man's nose. He hooked his arm around the man's neck and dragged him into the surf, wrestling his head under the water.

"Where?" he screamed. "Where did you find it?"

Two men from the crowd tackled Roger, and the drowning man crawled up onto the beach and into the crowd. Lunging out of the water and grabbing the knife, Roger collapsed on his knees in front of the dead animal. He raised the blade in the air and plunged it into the dark skin, spurting blood across his chest. He wiggled the knife free with both hands and lifted it, pounding the flesh again, wrenching the handle down the side of the carcass and into the sand, weeping.

24

Water dripped off the eaves of the main building of the hotel and fell into puddles blinking on the ground. Roger and Pepe jogged down the back steps and into the rain.

"It's too early, señor. They only get up in the afternoon. It's not the best thing to do so early in the morning. It's like opening a can of sleeping worms."

Roger splashed through the water, staring ahead. "Just translate. That's all you have to do, Pepe. Just translate."

"But I'm telling you. They don't like the cock-a-doodle-doo."

At the first house in town, a pack of dogs huddled underneath a warped table in the rain. Two men with machetes glanced at Roger and vanished into the bushes, carrying sacks flattened over their shoulders.

A door opened on a porch; a bucket of water swooshed into the street.

With a pile of bodies wrapped in canvas on its prow, the red and black Colombian boat squeaked against the pier. Beer bottles stood on the dock collecting rain. Roger stopped in front of the bowsprit.

"Hey," he called. "Where's Salvador?"

A tattooed arm stirred from the canvas.

"Señor," said Pepe. "It's not a good idea. It's better to wait."

Roger walked to the stern of the boat. "Hey. Anybody here? Hello."

"We can come back in the afternoon."

He beat on the hull with his fist. "Hey, Salvador."

A hatch lifted, and a woman's voice whimpered inside the boat. The bald-headed man stuck his head out and squinted in the rain.

"*¿Qué?*"

"Tell him I want to speak to Salvador."

"It's too early," said Pepe. "He's sleeping."

"Just tell him."

Pepe looked at the bald man and then back at Roger.

"Just tell him, Pepe."

"*Con permiso. El señor desea hablar con Salvador.*"

"*Ocupado,*" growled the man.

"Busy, señor. We can come back tomorrow."

"Tell him it's business," said Roger.

"It's not the time for business."

"Just tell him. It's business."

The bald man listened to Pepe, shucked phlegm from his throat, and spit in the water. His head sank below and he closed the hatch.

When the cover reopened, a hand jutted out and waved. Roger and Pepe climbed aboard and went down into the main cabin, where Salvador staggered, raking his fingers through his hair and buttoning his frayed shorts. The Colombian threw his body onto the bench behind the table and picked up an opened beer bottle, pouring the remains into his mouth and sloshing the liquid from cheek to cheek. He slapped the bottle down on the table and sprayed the dregs on the floor, froth scudding between the floorboards.

"*¿Comprar o vender?*" he grunted.

Roger and Pepe sat down. Drizzle blew through the open hatch.

"To buy or to sell?" said Pepe.

"Sell."

Salvador scratched his chest and belched.

"What you have?" said Pepe.

"Cocaine."

The girl in the back moaned.

"For this he cuts off our skin like a potato."

"Tell him I have some cocaine."

Pepe shook his head. "*El señor dice, desea vender . . . cocaína.*"

"*Ay,*" gasped the girl. "*Ay, querido.*" The side of Salvador's face twitched. He leaned forward and shouted down the hallway.

"*¿Cuánto cuesta?*"

"How much is the cost, señor?"

"Ask him if he bought it from my father."

Raindrops ticked on the roof of the cabin. Pepe

blotted his forehead with his sleeve and translated.

"*No,*" answered Salvador.

"Ask him how much he wants to pay."

"*¿Cuánto desea pagar?*"

"*Diez mil por un kilo.*"

"Ten thousand for the kilo," said Pepe. "Señor, you know it's not on the up and up to do this thing? If the *guardia . . .*"

"Ask him how much he wants to buy."

"*¿Cuánto desea comprar?*"

"*¿Cuánto tiene?*"

"He says, 'How much you have?'"

"Enough to cover the table."

Pepe winced. He tapped on the table and spoke while the girl in the back moaned.

"*Diez kilos,*" answered Salvador.

"He wants *diez* kilos, señor. Ten."

"Ask him where it comes from."

The girl shrieked.

"Where what comes from?" said Pepe.

"The cocaine."

"Señor, you mean, we're doing this and you don't have the cocaine?"

"I want to know where my father got it."

"Señor Ben?"

"Just translate."

Pepe spoke to the Colombian, who shook his head.

"He doesn't know where it comes from, señor."

"Tell him I'll pay for the information. I'll sell him the ten kilos for whatever he wants."

"*Ay,*" cried the girl. "*Sigue.*"

Salvador stood up and bent across the table, yelling down the hallway. The girl yelled back and gasped, and Salvador slumped in the booth with his cheek quivering again. "*San Blas*," he said.

"Where?"

"*¿Cuál isla?*" said Pepe.

"*Cuando tenga la cocaína,*" said the Colombian. "*Por mil dólares.*"

"He says the San Blas Islands. He tells you the name of the island when he gets the cocaine. For one thousand dollars."

"Ask him what he wanted to sell me the first time we came here."

"*¿Qué deseaba vendernos la primera vez?*"

"*Armas,*" said Salvador. He rose and looked down the hallway.

"Guns," said Pepe.

"Not cocaine?"

"He says 'guns.' I think it's better if we believe him. Please, señor."

Roger took a breath and nodded. "Tell him I'll bring the stuff tonight."

Pepe spoke and Roger stood up and held out his hand. The Colombian spit on the floor and walked toward the rear cabin.

On the way back to the hotel, the sky thundered. All afternoon Roger sat in a corner of the restaurant watching the rain splatter against the louvers and run down the inside of the glass. A gray mist filled the channel and covered the mainland from view.

At dusk a tube of sunlight passed through the haze,

tingeing the edges crimson and pink and falling on the horizon in an oval. The rain stopped and snips of thin silver clouds threaded low above the sea. Out on the reef floated a canoe with poles spoked over its sides and lanterns burning at the ends. A man sat in the boat, gazing into the water.

Roger untied the skiff from the hotel pier and rowed to his father's yacht. Into a burlap bag he loaded the cocaine, tying the neck with a string and lowering it into the skiff. He rowed into the channel, oarlocks plinking, barbs of jute pricking his legs. The floodlights of the great white church lined up behind the pier, and he angled toward the town, slowing the oars.

At the stern of the black boat, Salvador rested a foot on the railing and sucked on a cigarette. The bald man stood at his side, uncrossing his arms and pointing a dagger toward the water. The skiff drifted closer, and Roger clunked the oars into the boat and stood up, grabbing onto a dock line and pulling himself to the schooner. The bald man reached over and yanked the bag away, hauling it up on deck and lancing open its side. Salvador's cigarette hissed in the water.

Shoving a finger through the slit, the greasy Colombian held up a speck of white powder to his nose and snorted. The gold tooth twinkled. A paper bag dropped into the bottom of the skiff, and Roger picked it up and looked at the bills.

"Where?" he said. "Where in the San Blas?"

Salvador frowned.

"The San Blas," said Roger.

The bald sailor twirled the knife in his hand, squeezing the handle. Roger sat down in the skiff.

"Where? Please."

"*Corazón de Jesús,*" said Salvador.

"*Cor . . . a . . .*"

"*Corazón de Jesús.*"

The bald man patted his chest with the dagger and smirked, stooping over the rail. Roger pushed off from the boat and picked up the oars.

"*Cor . . . a . . . zón?*"

Salvador nodded.

"*De Je . . . sús?*"

The two Colombians laughed as Salvador rubbed a hand on the bald man's head. "*¿De Je . . . sús?*" he scoffed. "*¿De Je . . . sús?*"

25

"Heart?" said Roger.

The Indian bobbed his head once and slapped the throttle to the side of the canoe, veering the dugout through a pass in the reef. "*Corazón.*"

"Heart of Jesus?"

The Indian dipped his head again. His black bangs flopped in the wind. Sweat shined on his chest.

Around the bay, a few feet above sea level, dozens of coral islets lay. Fishing nets drying on poles staked the shores. A young boy on a beach pulled down his shorts and arching his back, urinated in the sand. With golden nose rings dangling from their nostrils and scarves of orange-vermilion draped atop their heads, a pair of women paddled a canoe toward the mainland.

The Indian motored around the corner of a sand spit

and ran the boat up on a beach clogged with thatched
huts. Clasping a bundle of embroidered squares in her
arms, a woman in an orange skirt and a red blouse
dashed out of a shack. Trinkets and colored beads
wound up her legs. Rows of silver discs clanked against
her chest.

"*Mola?*" she said, halting in front of Roger and
holding up a square. She tilted her head sideways. A
gold ring hung from her nose. "*Mola?*"

He got out of the canoe. The woman tucked the
piece of material under her arm and unfurled another.

"Heart of Jesus?" he asked the man.

The Indian nodded.

"Is there someone here who knew my father? Ben
Lord. He had a hotel."

Standing shoulder-high to Roger, the two Indians
stared up at him.

"Is there someone who remembers him?"

The man walked off down the beach, turning inland.
Roger followed as the Indian woman hugged her bundle
of material and jostled at his elbow.

The three strode down a corridor lined with huts
and stick fences. A swarm of children raced ahead in
the dirt, yelping. Through the gaps in their stick gates,
women in red and orange flagged squares of cloth and
clucked at Roger, their voices guggling in their throats.
Heads peered out of open windows. An albino woman
with black and yellow beads coiled around her ankles
and up her calves squirmed through the pack of children and waved a blouse in Roger's face.

"*Mola? Mola?*"

He kept walking.

"Fifty dollars," said the albino, her pupils shining pink. "Cheap."

The short man went through a gate and into a sandy yard, stopping in front of a doorless hut. Inside, a woman squatted by a fire, stirring coals with a branch and singing in another language. Her body rocked back and forth to the rhythm of her monotone as she dipped a hand into a gourd and sprinkled powder on the fire, sparking the flames. From a hammock near the back window, a leg dangled.

The short man and Roger, along with the gang of children and the two women with the *molas,* entered the next hut. Clothes drooped from lines between the ceiling beams; bags of flour and rice lay splayed open on the dirt floor. Behind a table stacked with canned food, an old man in faded army fatigues stood on a chair, hands clasped behind his back, a gray fedora hat pushed down to his eyebrows, his shoulders lost in his jacket. The two Indians spoke to each other.

"His name is Franky Roosevelt," said the first Indian. "He remembers your father."

The old man on the chair gummed his lips.

"When was the last time you saw him?" asked Roger.

"A long time ago."

"A year? Two years?"

"Maybe."

"They had a hotel."

The man nodded.

"You know where it was?"

He lifted an arm toward the door, his long sleeve

falling down over his hand.

"On the next island?"

"Out there." The old Indian retucked his arm behind his back.

"Which one?"

He stared at Roger.

"You know why they left?"

The old man shook his head and nibbled on his bottom lip.

With their black hair cropped at their eyebrows, a line of charcoal painted down their noses, and eyes skewed off-center, a group of Indians watched from the door. A baby with blue beads around its wrists and a gold ring piercing its nose suckled a woman's breast.

"Do you know where they sell cocaine?" said Roger.

The old man mashed his lips together. A bat plummeted to the ground from the shadows of the coned roof. Several boys ran over and picked up the dead animal and carried it outside.

Roger touched the bundle the albino woman carried in her arms. "Do you have any of these?"

The old man called out to the back of the hut, and a woman scurried forward and stacked a pile of appliquéd squares on the table.

"I'll buy all of them," said Roger. "But I need some information."

The Indian flattened and dimpled his cheeks.

"I want to know where they sell the cocaine. I don't want to buy any. I don't want to make any trouble. I just want to know where they sell it."

"Eighty dollars each," said the man.

"How many?"

"Ten," said the woman.

Roger looked at the albino. "But hers are fifty."

Franky Roosevelt stepped off his chair and walked out the door. Roger paid the money to the woman and swooped up the material, hurrying outside with the swarm of chattering people, past the hut with the singing woman, and onto the path.

Dogs barked at the hikers. Women left their stick fences and shook their *molas,* heckling Roger and trailing him through the village to the beach. He got into the canoe with the old man and the first Indian, and they left the chirping throng standing on the shore, silver jewelry glinting in the sun, *molas* fluttering.

The dugout pitched across the bay toward the mainland with the old Indian sitting in the bow, staring at Roger. Sheets of rain drifted down the mountain ridges and over the jungle, spraying water on the trees. The canoe slid onto a patch of mud beside a marsh, and the two Indians and Roger climbed out and walked through the bushes and up a hill to a jumble of charred wood lying at the top.

"They grew the plants in the valley and brought their boat in here," said the old man.

"My father?"

The two Indians turned around and looked out at the islands in the bay. The old man clasped his hands behind his back. The gray fedora dripped.

"When the Spanish first came to our islands, our people ran into the hills and hid for a hundred years. We heard stories about them from the north. But there is only disease in these hills. Half our people died of fever. When we saw that the Spanish ships couldn't get past the reefs, we came back to our islands. We found the missionaries waiting for us like hungry birds, building churches.

"Now the Spanish come by plane, like you, and bring radios and teach us another language and put a flag on our islands and call us Panamanians. I ran away to the canal when I was fourteen and worked on a freighter going to San Francisco. I know how you think.

"Your father was not welcome here, and others are not welcome. You tell us what to do and what to believe, what is right and what is wrong. These things are not good for our people.

"If we live alone, we live in peace. For this, we never say our real names or the names of our islands. The name of something has its spirit, and once the name is known, it can be owned by another."

"Was my father selling cocaine?"

"They came at night."

"What about the hotel? Why did they leave?"

"These are things you have in your world that we do not have in ours. We told him to go."

"What about the powerboat?"

The rain beat harder on the trees on the mountain-side.

"It's small enough to make it in here, isn't it?"

The two Indians turned and started down the hill.

"You ever see them with guns?" called Roger. "Were they selling guns?"

The two Indians disappeared through the bushes, and Roger stood alone in the ruins overlooking the islands, ashes exploding into clouds at his feet in the rain.

26

Roger stepped out of the elevator and into the marble alcove, setting his duffel bag down on the floor and pressing a button on a brass plate on the wall. The doorbell chimed. He waited and pushed the button again.

Gloria peeked through the glass with a pink towel snugged around her body. "Roger? It's you?" She opened the door. "Surprise. You come to say hello."

"I'm leaving."

"Leaving where?"

"Sorry to bother you. I was wondering if there's any more money in my parents' account so I can buy a ticket." He unzipped the bag and pulled out the corner of a *mola*. "I can leave you some of these."

"Roger, you go to the San Blas and you don't tell me? I could go with you. Come in. Forgive me the way

I'm dressed. Why are you leaving? You hear what happened to Señor Dutch?"

Roger entered the room and put the bag on a chair.

"Pepe says it's for the cocaine. They took him away."

"Who?"

"The *guardia*. They took him to the jail." She retucked a corner of the towel in her cleavage.

"They found the cocaine on the boat?"

"Pepe didn't say the boat. Only the *guardia* comes and finds the cocaine and takes Señor Dutch. Terrible, no?" She straddled the armrest of the sofa. "You just come back from the San Blas?"

"Where'd they take him?"

"Here. To the prison."

The blind maid walked through the room carrying a stack of sheets folded in her arms. She went down the hallway with her sandals slapping back and forth between the tile and the soles of her feet.

"What do we do?"

"Maybe pay them some money."

"And the trial?"

"What trial?"

"The trial," said Roger. "With the judge."

Gloria massaged a drop of water into her thigh. "Sometimes there's a judge. But then we have to pay for him, too. It's better to pay when it's only the general."

"But he didn't do anything. It's not his cocaine."

"Then why is he in jail?"

Roger looked at a lamp on an end table and then back at Gloria.

"Don't you know anyone who can help?"

"There's only the soldiers. But they're pigs." She feigned a spit in the air. "I hate them."

"What about someone in the government?"

"The soldiers are the government."

The footsteps of the blind maid dragged back down the hallway, and Roger walked outside to the veranda and over to the rail. Sunlight glared on the water. Sea gulls sharpened their beaks on the rocks below. Gloria crept up behind him and rested her chin on his shoulder, taking his hand and feeding it inside her towel.

He went to the other end of the veranda, and she followed him and took his hand. He pulled it away.

"What's wrong? You don't want to feel anything? You're too good to feel it?"

He inhaled and pushed the air out through his mouth as he ground the heels of his fists into his eyelids and rubbed his hands down the side of his face. "Shit."

"The shit what?" she said.

"Shit. Just shit. Is the hotel broke? Does it make any money?"

"Enough to pay the bills."

"Then why would he sell cocaine?"

"Señor Dutch?"

"My father."

"It's Señor Dutch."

"No. My father. I saw it on his boat."

"I don't believe it. It's somebody else."

Roger shook his head. "They're dead, you know."

"Who?"

"Jesus Christ, Gloria. My parents."

He went into the living room and picked up his bag and walked to the door. A vase of flowers shattered the plate glass panel.

"You're an asshole," she yelled. "What do you care who's dead and who's alive? What do you care?"

He walked outside and pushed the button for the elevator. The door opened and he got on.

27

The metal door slammed shut. A rod clicked. Foot-steps echoed down the hallway and faded away. Roger stood for a moment and extended an arm in the dark-ness, scraping his knuckles against a wall. He sniffed.

"Anybody here?"

"Kid?"

"Dutch? That you?"

"What the hell you doing here?"

"I told them it was my father's cocaine."

"You're a dumb ass. What the hell for?"

"It's not yours. I had to do something."

"You're fucking crazy."

"What's that smell?"

"I put some shit down there for the guard."

Roger took a step forward and wiped off his shoes against the wall. "You okay, Dutch?"

"I'm great."

"What happened?"

"I goddamned got arrested."

"But how?"

"The boat was leaking. I went over to patch it up, and de León showed up with the whole goddamned National Guard."

"It's not your boat."

"No shit."

"The cocaine belongs to my father. I saw the place in the San Blas where he made it."

"So what?"

"He knew the place. It's next to where the hotel was."

"What difference does it make?"

"You knew."

"I didn't know it was on the sailboat. He always kept it on the other one."

"What for? Why'd he have to sell cocaine?"

"He traded it for guns."

"Why?"

"To get more guns."

"But de la Cruz gave him money."

"And they always ran out. I did it for a while, taking my boat back and forth to Colombia, until they stopped paying me. That's when your old man started trading the coke."

"But what for? It's not even his country."

"People got all kinds of crazy reasons."

"Why'd they have to get involved in this? What's de la Cruz going to do? Can't they just have an election?

Why's it have to be like this?"

"That's the way it is, that's all."

"You think it's okay to sell cocaine and buy guns?"

"You didn't bring anything to drink, did you?"

Roger crept ahead a couple of steps and crouched against the wall. A sliver of light shone at the bottom of the door. Something thumped against the wall above his head. Wings hummed in front of his face. He leaned forward and swiped at the air, one of his knees dropping onto the concrete, his hand falling onto a slab of cold flesh. He scrambled back against the wall.

"Jesus. What's that?"

"Sounded like one of those cockroaches," said Dutch.

"On the floor." He stretched a leg out and nudged the bundle. "Jesus Christ. A body."

"Another one?"

"Another?"

"There's one over here next to me."

"Just lying there?"

"Yeah."

"Dead?"

"It's not moving."

"Who are they?"

"How the hell should I know?"

"They're just lying here?"

"It's a fucking prison, kid."

Roger sagged against a corner. "They'll just keep us here? They just do whatever they want? Don't we have a lawyer?"

Dutch walked across the cell and unzipped his pants.

"Yeah. Here's our lawyer hard at work." He pissed into the crack of light under the door. "Ain't that the fucking history of the world, kid?"

28

Light flooded into the small room. Roger raised an arm and shielded his eyes. A tall, thin soldier with a club entered the cell.

"*Mierda,*" shouted the soldier. He stomped his boot on the concrete and rushed inside, kicking Dutch in the chest and smearing excrement over the bony man's shirt and pants. He pointed the tip of his club at Roger.

"*Usted. Venga.*"

"He wants you to go with him," groaned Dutch.

The soldier cracked the stick into Dutch's groin and grappled on to the front of Roger's shirt, dragging him over a corpse and into the corridor, sending maggots panicking toward the walls and out the door. The vault crashed shut; the bolt pinged into its bracket.

The tall soldier chipped at Roger's shoulder blades with the end of his club, shoving him down the hallway and into an office, where Roger collapsed on his knees in front of a large desk. The soldier cuffed him on the side of the head and left the room, shutting the door. Humming behind the desk, a man in a tan uniform stopped writing and laid down his pen. A black and white nameplate on his chest read CORONEL VARGAS.

"*Buenos días, señor,*" said the man.

Roger rocked back and forth on his knees, hugging his elbows.

"Did we disturb your sleep?" The colonel chuckled, shaking his rounded shoulders up and down and primping the ends of his mustache with a finger. He took a piece of paper and stood up, walking around to the front of the desk and sitting on the corner. He nodded toward a chair and Roger crawled over to it, pulled himself up, and sat down. One of the colonel's boots circled in the air above the floor.

"You are Roger Lord?"

He looked up at the colonel.

"And you have confessed to having cocaine on your father's boat at Isla Grande?"

"It's not my cocaine. I explained that before."

Colonel Vargas set the paper down on the desk.

"Do you know where you are, señor?"

Roger nodded.

The colonel laughed. A row of gold fillings gleamed in his mouth. "Where?"

"In prison."

"Correct. You are in prison. But you are in prison in Panama, in the *Centro de La Guardia Nacional*, in Panama City, in the Republic of Panama. And how long have you been here?"

"One day?"

"And are you alone in this prison?"

"No."

The black boot circled. "Good. You are very smart. And how many are with you?"

"Dutch. And there's two dead bodies."

"Two," laughed the colonel. "Only two?"

"I think so."

"It is very difficult to count, no? There are some, a few, a very few, who leave this prison more or less alive. But there are many others who become sick and cannot move. Maybe it's the food. Have you tried the soup yet?" The colonel smiled. "And some we forget about until we need the space. Our system of accounting is not so good like in your country. Things are always being lost. Sometimes we think someone is here, but when we look, we cannot find him. Many of our men, you know, they cannot even write their own names."

"What do you want?"

The boot stopped moving. "It's a very serious offense, my friend. And the punishment is also very serious. But we are prepared to make a kind of agreement. A deal, no?"

The colonel picked up the paper from his desk. "It is true that your parents have been missing now for three months?"

Roger stared at the colonel.

"And the hotel on the island is owned by you?"

"What?"

Colonel Vargas handed the piece of paper to Roger. "The title of ownership to the hotel. It says you are the beneficiary in case of your parents' death."

"Where'd you get this?"

"From our good friend, *Sargento* de León." The colonel folded his hands in his lap and smiled. "I have been thinking about your situation to see if there is anything we can do to make it better. You know, the laws in our country are very strict for drug dealers. But, I think we may be able to help you. In fact, you and your friend could be free today. Of course, you must be willing to do something for us in return."

"What?"

"Sign over the hotel and agree to leave the country forever."

"You want the hotel?"

"We want you to leave."

Roger glanced at the document. "What if my parents aren't dead?"

"After three months, señor, they can be." The colonel leaned back and plucked the pen from the top of his desk.

"What about my things at the island? What about Dutch's boat?"

"First, you can sign the paper. Then, if you wish, you may go to the island and bring the boat to the canal. Your friend, of course, will have to stay with us. He will be the deposit, no?" The colonel offered the pen to Roger.

"Then can you move him to an empty cell?"

"At least," snickered the colonel, "we will try to

move some of the bodies."

The black boot began to swing as he bent forward, pointing to a space at the bottom of the page. "Here, my friend, is your freedom."

29

The front door of the house opened, and Moonshot walked down the steps to a copper tube rising out of the mud into a crook. Sunlight yellowed the plaster walls of the building. She spread out a towel on a rock and lifted her dress up over her shoulders, folding it in her arms and placing it on the rock beside the towel. She turned the handle on the staff. Liquid gurgled out the end of the pipe and splattered on the ground. She flattened her palms in the stream, water skipping up to her face and chest and pearling on the sides of her breasts.

From a space between the trees, Roger turned and crept down the path to the beach, where he sat in the sand and watched the white caps toss at sea. Waves crashed near the shore and spray netted his face. He closed his eyes.

"Dreaming?"

Moonshot sat down beside him, the sleeves of her dress splotched with water.

"You were waiting for me?" she said. "At the house?" She bent her legs up like his, put her chin on her knees, and stared out at the ocean.

"You heard about the cocaine? I had to sign over the hotel. I have to leave." He closed his eyes and lay back in the sand. "I'm sorry."

"Why?"

"I don't know. I'm just sorry."

She took his hand and tugged on it until he got to his feet, and she led him across the beach to the jungle, telling him not to ask, drawing him through the vines and branches to the mountain. She climbed, turning around and calling him up the slope.

At the top of the hill, a path dropped down the other side to a clearing with some trees on a ledge. The wind chilled his face. Sea birds arched out their wings and twisted their necks from side to side, cawing, floating in the updraft. Moonshot walked to the half-circle of trees and bunched her hair back into a ponytail as she looked up at the leaves.

"Aren't they beautiful?" she said. "*Loa* trees. The only ones on the island."

She stroked the side of a trunk and broke off a piece of bark, snapping it under her nose and rubbing the powder into her fingers. She opened her hands in front of him.

"Smells like cinnamon," he said.

"I remember one time my mother gave me some

medicine made from the bark." She lifted her hands again to her face. "And my grandfather told me about a man who died here, setting fire to one of the trees. He made a cut from the top of the tree all the way down to the bottom. Then he set fire to it and stood over there." She walked into the sun. "Facing the wind."

"Why?"

"The smell. They say that when it burns, it's the smell of heaven."

"What happened to him?"

"The tree fell." She laughed to herself. "My grandfather would always say, 'The wind that blows the smoke of the *Loa* also blows the tree.'"

Roger touched a trunk.

"I want to smell one," she said.

"A tree?"

She paced down the row.

"Why don't you just take a branch?" He dug his fingernails into the bark. "Anyway, it's too wet. It won't burn."

"The tops are dry. And the juice will make the fire spread. You can use a rock."

He picked up a stone and scratched it against the skin. "See." Sap oozed out the gash. "Too soft. It won't burn."

"A straight line," she said. "The juice has to run all along the cut." She cupped her hands around her nose.

"You have matches?"

She nodded.

He looked up at the branches spiked in the air and shoved the stone into his pocket. "Anyway, nothing's going to happen."

He grabbed on to a limb and walked his feet up the trunk, curling his legs around the lowest branch and swinging his body up and over as he hugged the tree. Chips of bark crumbled in his hands; dust drifted to the ground. He climbed to the next branch, where the pointed ends of the leaves stippled his arms, dotting his skin with droplets of blood.

"There's fruit," he said. "Looks like plums or large cherries."

He pulled a cluster of twigs over and stripped them with his hand, raining leaves and white flowers and pieces of fruit on the ground. Moonshot knelt in the grass and picked up the red balls, cradling them in the folds of her dress.

He climbed to the top of the tree and hung, swaying above the ledge. Gripping the crown with one hand, he eased the stone out of his pocket and pressed it against the bark. Sap poured over the furrow and gummed his hands and shirt. He shinnied down, stopping to scrape, sliding some more, etching the line lower and lower. On the ground he made the final cuts and slung the stone over the cliff.

She handed him a book of matches.

"It won't burn," he said. "It's too wet."

She shifted the front of her dress from one hand to two, fruit piled in the scoop, her lap smeared red with pulp. He lit a match and touched it against the sap. The light fizzled.

"No good," he said.

"Try again. It has to be higher."

He struck another match and held it up over his head, and it blew out in the wind. He tried a third, and the sap sparkled and caught fire. A line of orange flared up the trunk. He backed away, and they went to the other side of the clearing and stood, watching the bark steam.

"I don't smell it," he said.

Moonshot sat down facing the tree and chose a piece of fruit from the pile on her dress. He sat beside her, and she brushed off the fruit with her hand and put it to his lips. He took a bite. The tree crackled. Smoke streamed toward the mountain.

"Do you smell it now?"

He swallowed and inhaled. "Mint and cinnamon." The tree flamed. "How long do we have?"

"A few minutes. Until the ends turn white."

She finished the fruit and threw the pit into the bushes and lay on her back, closing her eyes. Sparks shot off the tree limbs. A bouquet of white flowers melted in the heat. Roger leaned back on his elbows.

"It sure doesn't look like heaven," he said. "It looks more like hell."

"Don't look," she said.

He closed his eyes and lay down and felt her fingers slide down his arm and squeeze his hand.

A soft tickling covered his face. Twigs popped in the air. He raised a hand and looked up as the tree, a shower of sparks and glowing red leaves, screamed toward him.

He grabbed Moonshot and rolled her over, covering her with his body. The tree slammed into the ground and bounced, whooshing out heat and flame and torching the shrubs at the back of the clearing. The trunk rumbled to the edge of the cliff and fell off, shooting smolder and ash into the air.

"You all right?"

She stood up. The tree stump and the bushes around them blazed. The smell of mint blew over the clearing as branchlets and splinters lay afire on the grass. She walked to the ledge, where the wind blew her dress back through her legs and whipped her hair behind her.

"So fast," she said.

"It could've killed us." He got up and brushed at the hairs singed on his arms and went over to the ledge. The black trunk tossed against the rocks at the bottom.

"Are you sorry?" she said.

"About what?"

"Anything."

"I'm sorry we came here."

"But nothing happened." She turned to him. "There's nothing to be afraid of, is there, Roger?"

"No," he said. "Nothing."

Thousands of coals at their feet peppered the ground red, and overhead, the sea birds lifted up and floated away in the wind.

"Let's go back," he said. "It's time to go."

30

Roger wandered down the dirt road in town and climbed the steps of a white stuccoed building with the words *La Guardia Nacional* printed in black letters on the front wall. He went through the opened door and into the one room, where Sergeant de León sat perched in a chair behind a desk with his eyes closed, his feet crossed on a drawer handle, his head resting on his shoulder.

Roger stopped in front of the desk, and the sergeant jerked his head up, blinking his eyes. A toothpick slipped out the corner of his mouth.

"It's the smuggler?" The sergeant picked the toothpick off his T-shirt and stuck it back in his mouth. "You come looking for your friend?"

"What friend?"

"Señor Smith."

"He's here?"

"Only a few parts." Sergeant de León arched his back and folded his hands on his stomach. "We found the arm this morning on the beach. The one with the tattoo of the heart. Later, we found a very small penis in the sand. We are not sure if it's his, but with the arm there is no mistake."

"A penis?"

"I don't think it fell off."

"You're joking, right?"

"I don't make jokes about a man's penis unless I can say it to his face. What do you want?"

"You found his arm?"

"The tattoo is the same. You want to see it or you come for something else?"

"Why'd you arrest Dutch?"

"The people saw the white powder on the beach and they came to tell me. I'm the *guardia,* no? I must follow the law and do the right thing." The sergeant reached back and clasped his hands behind his head. "I'm sorry about the hotel."

"It wasn't his cocaine."

"It's your father's."

"No."

"Then it's yours."

"No."

Sergeant de León shrugged his shoulders. "I'm sorry, señor. I'm only doing my job."

"What happened to my parents?"

The sergeant clamped down on the toothpick and shook his head.

"That's your job. You're the police. You're supposed to find out who killed them. You think it was Colombians?"

The toothpick disappeared in the sergeant's mouth and came out the other corner. "It's possible. Who can trust them?"

"The Indians from the San Blas?"

"The Cunas? I never thought of this one. It's possible, too. The people here, they say it's the spirits."

"And what do you think?"

"I am only one man, señor. If I see someone, I will arrest them."

"You believe in the spirits?"

"Sometimes I believe and sometimes I don't believe."

"What's that mean?"

"It means, señor, that life is full of strange things, and the best we can do is the best we can do."

"You think the spirits killed my parents?"

"It's always possible."

"Shit."

The sergeant's chair slammed to the floor. "Sí, señor. Shit. The shit is everywhere. Even on a beautiful island like this one." He jerked the pistol from his holster and aimed it at the window, fanning a palm across the hammer. Chips of wood spiraled off the sill. An empty vase exploded, scattering pieces of clay across the floor.

"Shit, *Americano*? This is the shit." The sergeant wagged his pistol in the air.

Roger left the office and walked down the steps as people in the street peered at the building and watched him tramp away. He walked through the town to the trail and followed it through the jungle to the hotel and out onto the beach of the gutted shark. He entered his parents' bungalow and pulled a sheet off the bed, stacking it with the photographs from the walls. Tying the four corners together, he hauled the sack outside and dragged it across the sand toward the hotel, glass and wood rattling against his leg.

In the restaurant he dropped the bundle at the door and went to the bar, where Pepe opened a bottle of beer and set it on a napkin.

"You're leaving, señor?"

Roger nodded and drank from the bottle.

"Who's going to run the hotel, Pepe?"

"*Sargento* de León."

"Him?" Roger took another swallow. "You heard about Smith?"

Pepe nodded. "He arrived last night, but I didn't see him after dinner."

"Alone?"

"Sí, señor."

"An arm, Pepe. Jesus Christ. And his penis?"

The fat man sighed and wiped the counter.

"You think it's the same thing that happened to my parents?"

"It's the sixty-four thousand dollars question, no?"

"My father was buying guns and selling cocaine . . . with Smith."

"I never liked this Smith."

"You think de León could have killed them?"

"What for?"

"Maybe he wants the hotel."

"But how can we know?"

Roger sipped at the beer, and Pepe took away the napkin and put down a new one.

"The Cunas ever come down this far?"

"Only I see them sometimes on the banana boats going to the canal. They're dangerous, but only in the San Blas."

"The people on the island think it was the spirits."

"Sí, señor."

Roger shook his head. "I know it was my father's fault. He got mixed up in all this."

"Maybe he had no choice."

"Of course he had a choice. He could always go back to the States."

"Maybe he doesn't want to go."

"Why not?"

"Maybe he likes it here."

"Here?"

"The people are happy. We have little money and the work is hard, but there's music all the time. Sing, dance, make love. It's a life, no?"

"No," said Roger.

"Maybe we can't do all the things like you because we aren't rich. It's the money that makes you free. If I have the money, I would be free, too." Pepe leaned closer to the bar. "But with the money or without the money, inside, I'm happy. This, señor, is the difference."

"But why would my father get involved in all this?"

"I'm telling you. Maybe he had no choice."

"There's always a choice."

Pepe dried his hands with the towel. "You are the true gringo."

"The true gringo?"

"You understand only the one way to live and everything else is wrong. I think it's the American disease. Your father was a good man. Why don't you look at that? If something he does you don't like, you should believe him and not spit on the people who bring you into the world."

"You don't understand, Pepe."

"Maybe no, señor. But I know your father was a good man."

Roger swallowed the last of his beer and walked out, grabbing the bag at the door. He crossed the sand to the pier and threw the bag and some plastic water jugs into the skiff. He climbed in and started the motor, racing out past the reef and into the open channel, the plastic bottles clunking together in the bottom of the boat.

Halfway between the island and the mainland he idled the engine and crawled forward to the white bundle in the bow, rolling it up to his waist. The boat slowed and pitched in the swells. He gathered the sack up onto his shoulder and heaved it over the side into the water. Glass shattered. Air gurgled out the corners of the sheet.

He took out his mother's wedding ring from a pocket in his pants and squeezed it in his hand. He slid it on and off his little finger and reached back with his foot and kicked down the gear lever. He held the gold ring out over the side of the boat as the skiff moved away.

He let go.

31

Roger ran the skiff up on the sand on the mainland and tossed out the plastic containers. The dark boy sprinted down the beach in the dusk, holding his pants up at the waist.

"*Papá, Papá,*" shouted the boy. "*Papá.* All night." He pointed at the channel.

Roger climbed out of the skiff.

"Fishing. Last night."

"I thought he doesn't go out there after dark."

"*Enfermo,*" said the boy. "Sick. Crazy."

"He's probably tired."

"No." The boy shook his head. "Very sick. Very crazy."

Roger gathered up the containers and took them to the hand pump behind the old man's shack. He filled the jugs with fresh water, and the boy screwed on the caps. They carried the jugs back toward the beach. At the door of the shack, the boy stopped and set down his containers in the dirt.

"Please," he said.

"What do you want me to do? I'm not a doctor."

The boy walked inside. Roger put down the jugs on the bench and followed the boy through the doorway.

They passed a smoldering fire in a pit and a wood table with three chairs. In a smaller room the pregnant woman sat in a corner with a baby on her lap. A painting of a black Christ on a cross hung on the wall above her head. The old man lay on a cot with a quilt snugged up under his white beard. He glared at the boy.

"*Son los soldados. Los soldados.*"

"What's he saying?" asked Roger.

"Soldiers. All day he says the same."

"Who's he talking about?"

"Sick," said the boy.

"Ask him who the soldiers are."

"*¿Qué soldados?*" asked the boy.

"*Son los soldados.*"

"*¿Quiénes son, Papá? ¿Quiénes?*"

The old man tugged at the boy's wrist and pulled him down to the bed. "*Los espíritus. Los espíritus con machetes.*"

"The spirits with machetes," said the boy.

"Machetes?"

"*Los ví anoche con un hombre. Los soldados lo mataron.*"

"He saw them kill a man last night."

"Who?"

The old man jerked the boy's arm. "*En su canoa próxima a la isla.*"

"Next to the island in the canoe," said the boy. "He's dreaming."

"What soldiers?"

"*¿Quiénes son los soldados, Papá?*"

The old man rolled his head from side to side.

"Did he see Sergeant de León?"

"*¿El sargento?*" said the boy.

"*Soldados.*"

"Soldiers. That's all he says all day. Soldiers."

Roger left the shack and ran with the jugs down the beach to the skiff, tumbling the containers inside the boat and pushing off into the channel. He plowed the skiff through the rollers to the island and tied up at his father's sailboat, climbing aboard and taking the revolver out of the cabinet in the galley, checking the bullets in their chambers. He climbed back into the skiff and rowed to shore.

He strode into town and mounted the steps of the sergeant's office. A woman's voice called out from across the street.

"He's dead."

Roger turned, lowering the gun.

"She's killed him," said the woman. She lifted the bottom of her dress and hurried down the street toward the path as more people chased behind her. Roger followed them into the jungle, clutching his pistol.

In front of the sergeant's house, a crowd of spectators jostled each other on the stairs and around the door, craning their necks to see inside. Sunset glowed orange on the building. Roger pushed his way through the crowd and went up the steps to the opened door. Inside, a line of blood trickled out from behind a sofa and curved across the floorboards to a knothole in the floor near the leg of a chair. The toe of a black boot lay in a pool of blood, the heel slanted in the air. Roger raised his pistol and walked in.

Sergeant de León's body stretched face down across the floor behind the sofa, an arm bent up on his back, the fingers curled in the palm. On his crimson T-shirt a knife handle jutted up, the point rammed in under a shoulder blade. Roger nudged the sergeant's head with his foot. Blood oozed out the mouth; a toothpick floated in the stream.

From the half-opened doorway in the next room, a creak echoed through the house. Specks of green and yellow flickered in the shadows. Twilight grayed the room. Roger lit a kerosene lamp and carried it toward the noise, his gun held out in front of him. He kicked open the door. Liquid tapped into a puddle on the floor.

"She's dead," said a voice from outside. "She's killed herself."

He lifted the lamp. Her hands dangling at her sides, a rope soaked red around her neck, Moonshot swung from a ceiling beam. Green and yellow beetles ticked at the glass cover on the kerosene lamp. Roger walked out of the room and past the corpse of Sergeant de León, children's heads peeping through the open windows. He set the lamp on the floor next to the door and went outside.

"What happened?" said a voice.

"He's killed him," said another. "Look. There's the gun."

"No. It was Moonshot. She did it."

"Anyway," said an old man, "the colonel will come from the city. They'll kill a hundred this time."

Pepe stood in the mud at the bottom of the steps, fingering the edges of his apron. "What happened, señor? Are they dead? She killed him?"

Roger stared past the fat man and walked into the bushes, winding down the path to the beach. He wandered across the sand to the skiff and dragged the boat into the water and got in, sitting with the gun between his knees, drifting in the current.

"Señor Roger," called the fat man. "Señor Roger."

Roger crawled to the back of the boat and yanked the starting cord. The propeller sputtered and stopped.

"Señor Roger," shouted Pepe, waving the white apron from the beach. "There . . . is . . . no . . . chair."

He pulled the cord again.

"Señor Roger. The . . . chair. There . . . is . . . no . . . chair."

The engine started, and Roger looked at the beach and then at the gun, raising the weapon with both hands and firing into the sky until the hammer clicked twice. The skiff circled in front of the island. He hurled the pistol into the water and grabbed the rudder and steered toward Dutch's boat.

32

A blue supertanker emerged from the breakwater at the canal and headed out to sea with its bass horn howling. A flight of frigate birds swooped over the foam in the wake of the ship and glided to the breakwater, tucking their wings and landing on the rocks.

On Dutch's sailboat Roger pushed the starter button, and the motor hummed. He climbed up on the cabin top and released the mainsheet, dropping the mainsail and gathering it in. He lashed it to the boom with nylon strips he gripped between his teeth. A bell buoy clanked nearby. The boat tobogganed down a swell and slid into the calm of the harbor.

In front of the yacht club, a black man on the floating dock caught the lines to the boat and tied them off on bollards. Roger turned off the engine, and the man sat down on the dock, picking up a string and whirling it in the air above his head. A fish hook plopped into the water.

Pepe trampled down the floating ramp to the boat as Roger stepped out.

"I'm getting Dutch and we're leaving," said Roger.

Pepe shook his head. "All the people are in the church, señor. They're afraid. The *guardia* is everywhere on the island. They're the ones who killed the *sargento*."

"It was Moonshot."

"She kills the *sargento* and then she kills herself?"

"Yeah."

"But there's no chair. How can she do it if there's no chair?"

"What chair?"

"The chair to stand on."

"She kicked it away."

"Into the other room, señor? There was no chair in the room. Only the bed in the corner."

"Why would they kill de León?"

"For the hotel. For the money from the Colombians. Maybe they're selling the cocaine, too? The *coronel* can do anything. He's the brother of the *generalísimo*. Maybe they also killed Señor Ben and Mrs. Birdie. They're the wolves who look like the sheep but smell like the dogs."

Three soldiers in green fatigues strutted down the dock with automatic rifles slung over their shoulders. The fisherman slid the line through his fingers and pulled up the hook, spinning it with his wrist and throwing it back into the water. The three soldiers halted in front of the boat.

"Señor Lord?" said the first soldier.

"Where's Dutch?"

"We have orders that you must leave today."

"I need supplies."

The soldier shook his head. "Today."

"I have to wait for Dutch."

The first soldier flicked a hand behind him, and the other two soldiers went back up the ramp and returned with a wooden box, shifting it up and down between them as they stumbled over the boards. They hoisted the crate up onto the deck of the sailboat. A fish jumped into the air and slapped the water. The black fisherman tugged on his line and looked over at the box.

"What's this?" said Roger.

The three soldiers watched as he opened the lid.

Dutch lay on his back, his hands lashed together with rope and crossed on his stomach. Under his neck a red pool of blood stained the wood. Roger reached inside and parted the hair on the back of Dutch's head, worming a finger inside a hole at the base of the skull. Blood moistened his hand.

The fisherman snared the fish in his palm and squeezed its throat, opening the mouth and jerking out the hook. He threw the fish in a bucket and stood up, staring at the body. The fish skittered against the sides of the pail.

"*Vuelen las cuerdas,*" shouted the first soldier.

Pepe jumped onto the boat as the soldiers swung their rifles off their shoulders and shot through the lines, splattering the water with gunfire. A woman screamed from the yacht club. The black fisherman dropped onto the dock and covered his head.

Roger scrambled onto the stern of the boat. "You fucking bastards."

The first soldier wiped his lips with the back of his hand and kicked the fisherman's pail into the water as the sailboat drifted toward a row of freighters tied up at the fuel dock. Sailors leaned over the ships' railings and pointed down at the yacht. Roger turned on the engine and moved the boat forward.

"They shot him. The fucking bastards shot him."

"God is not looking," said Pepe.

Roger turned the boat toward the floating dock with the three soldiers standing on it and throttled the engine. Pepe dropped down on the deck in the stern, and the black fisherman crawled to the edge of the dock and slipped into the water as the soldiers raised their weapons. A burst of machine gun fire riddled the canvas cockpit cover over Roger's head. A patrol boat cut across his bow, mounted guns swiveling, shooting out more of the canvas awning. Roger idled the engine and spun the wheel, turning the sailboat away. The three soldiers on the dock cradled their rifles in their arms and laughed. The silver eyelets on their boots glistened in the sun.

"Steer the boat," said Roger.

Pepe pushed himself to his feet and took the wheel.

Roger went below and snatched Dutch's clothes and bottles from the V berth and the galley and brought them up on deck, kicking the lid closed on the coffin and dumping everything in his arms over the stern. The gunboat swerved through the debris, rattling off spurts of gunfire at the bottles, the soldiers cheering the sound of popping glass.

Swells rolled under the hull of the sailboat, swaying it from side to side before the breakwater. Roger's hand burned in the wind. He looked down at the red hole in his palm and hiked up his T-shirt and pulled it off his back, wrapping the cloth around the wound and staring at the gunboat as it trailed them through the breakwater and out to sea.

"Maybe they'll kill us when we get outside," said Pepe. "When God is not looking, who knows what they do?"

Roger walked forward to the cockpit and sat down, hugging his hand against his stomach. The patrol boat slowed and turned around, a machine gun spraying bullets across the water, a soldier on the control bridge crisscrossing his arms over his head, good-bye.

33

The mainsail hit the top of the mast with a clank and flared out in the wind, heeling the boat over on her side. Pepe held to the wheel. The wooden crate scraped across the deck, crashing into a cleat and tipping over. The corpse flopped out and smeared the deck with blood.

Roger fastened the halyard to the mast and went below, taking a sheet off a bunk and bringing it up on deck. He spread out the cloth beside the body and rolled the cadaver over twice, straightening the legs and tucking the sheet underneath.

From a storage locker in the stern, he hauled out an anchor chain and looped it around Dutch's ankles, crossing the body to the head and back down to the feet. He shackled an anchor to the waist and hooked the flukes under the chain.

Wiggling the corpse from side to side by its feet, he dragged it across the deck to an open space between two stanchions, scooting the legs over the edge until the knees bent and the chain around the feet cracked against the hull. He sat the body up and pushed. The sack plunged into the sea, disappearing in a hiss of white bubbles.

He lifted one end of the crate and set it on top of the lifeline at the stern, boosting the bottom up and heaving it over the side. The box splat on the water and floated away. He scooped up a bucket of saltwater from the ocean and swished it across the deck, scuffing at the red marks with his feet. The blood hit the rails and swilled through the scuppers.

The bucket he tossed in the storage locker and went to the cockpit and sat down, unwinding the T-shirt from his hand. A sliver of bone tumbled out of the wrapping and fell on the deck.

"Where we going, señor?" asked Pepe.

Roger covered the hole with the T-shirt again and closed his eyes, laying his head back against the cabin. Water rushed alongside the boat. "Florida."

"What about Isla Grande?"

"You can fly back."

"What about the people?"

"There's nothing to do."

"There is, señor."

"No." Roger opened his eyes and squinted, squeezing his hand to his stomach.

"If it was your country," said Pepe, "I would go back. They're people, señor. Like the people everywhere."

"It's a sick country with a sick government. I wish I never came."

"If we have a sickness, we must do something."

The boat pounded into a wave, spraying mist over the cockpit.

"There's nothing you can do."

"If you won't take me, señor, then I'll swim."

"Forty miles?"

Pepe took a seat cushion, letting the wheel spin, and walked to the back of the boat.

Roger grabbed the helm. "You can't swim there."

"With the help of God, señor." He stepped over the lifeline and leaned across the stern of the boat, swinging with one hand from the backstay.

"Pepe . . ."

The fat man jumped. Roger spun the wheel, and the boat turned through the wind, swinging the boom over the cabin. He tightened the mainsheet and sailed toward the white cushion in the water.

"Go on," shouted Roger. "Swim."

"I can't swim." The fat man clung to the cushion as the boat sailed past.

"Then you'll end up in Cuba," called Roger. "You want to go to Cuba?"

"I want to go to Isla Grande."

The boat turned around. Pepe kicked his legs in the water. "Take me back. Leave me there."

Roger angled the yacht upwind and coasted toward Pepe as the mainsail luffed. He hung a ladder over the side.

"Get on."

The fat man paddled to the boat. "We're going back?"

"Just get on."

Pepe hauled himself up the ladder with the cushion and lay down on the deck, shivering in the wind.

"What for? Why you want to go back there?"

Pepe gasped for air and brushed water off his face.

"There's other places," said Roger. "Why don't you go back to the city?"

"I want to go to Isla Grande."

"You'll forget."

"How can I forget?"

"There's nothing you can do there."

"If a woman says to leave her with a kiss, and you leave her without the kiss, she finds it with someone else. You lose the things that make you happy. I want to keep the things that make me happy."

Roger shook his head and pulled up the ladder and helped Pepe to the helm, setting the course and giving him the wheel. He lay down in the cockpit and rested his head in the corner, the gush of water against the hull vibrating through the boat to his skull. His hand throbbed. He gazed into the distance downwind and watched the wooden coffin with its lid blown open drifting on the sea.

34

Roger woke up as thunder cracked overhead. Wire halyards chimed against the mast in the wind. The boat lifted and dropped in the darkness.

"Storm," said Pepe. "*Chubasco.*"

The boat lashed into a wave, pitching spray through the holes in the cockpit awning. Pepe grappled with the wheel.

"The island, señor."

A sprinkle of white lights twinkled and vanished in the darkness. The hull smashed into another wave and climbed. The lights flashed again and the boat dipped into the black. Roger crawled onto the cabin top, lowering the mainsail and furling it as he clung to the mast with his good hand. Creeping back into the cockpit, he started the engine and took the helm.

Lightning exploded over the mountain ridges on the

mainland and lit the bay and a corner of Isla Grande. The boat wobbled down the middle of the channel, past the church, to the seaward side of the island. Froth blanketed the ocean. They drifted toward the cliffs.

"Take the dinghy," shouted Roger.

The fat man stumbled to the back of the boat and dumped the rubber raft over the transom with a rope. Roger swung the bow into the wind, stalling the yacht in front of the rocks.

"Hurry."

"I will not forget this, señor." Pepe climbed over the side and disappeared.

Lightning burst, flushing the island green. Roger piloted the boat toward the open sea.

Something bumped against the yacht. A scratch dragged the length of the hull and stopped at Roger's side. The tip of a shotgun jutted up. Hands clawed onto the railing. Heads rose. A group of bare-chested men stared into the cockpit, aiming their rifles at Roger. Two of the men scrambled aboard and tossed off a line, barking out commands in Spanish. The barrel of a shotgun jarred against Roger's ear. The other man took the wheel and steered the boat around the end of the island, towing a canoe.

A gang of soldiers in slickers stood on the pier in front of the town, automatic rifles strapped across their shoulders, raindrops pounding at their boots. They tied up the boat and swarmed on, going below, forcing open drawers and cabinets, smelling bottles, peering into bags. The barrel of the shotgun chopped at Roger's neck.

"*Vamos,*" said the bare-chested man.

Roger stepped into the rainstorm and walked to the end of the pier, where mud and water flowed across the street toward the beach. They slushed through the town and entered the jungle under the roar of leaves, the shotgun jolting against Roger's spine. On the porch of a bungalow next to the hotel, a group of soldiers crouched together, smoking cigarettes.

"*¿Qué tienes, Zorro?*" shouted one of the soldiers.

"*Pescado fresco,*" said the man behind Roger.

The soldiers laughed.

"*Qué lástima que no sea una ninfa,*" called another. He drew the curved lines of a woman in the air with his hands. The soldiers laughed again and smoked, the tips of their cigarettes glowing red.

"*¿El capitán?*" asked the man with Roger.

"*Adentro.*"

One of the soldiers jabbed a thumb at the bungalow. The gunman pushed Roger up the stairs and inside the room.

Four soldiers pinned a naked girl across a bed, each man stretching one of her limbs to the side and pressing it against the mattress. A fifth man, his pants jammed down to his ankles, knelt between the girl's legs, humping. A pair of white underpants bulged from the girl's mouth, a corner of the material blowing across her lips as she huffed through her nose. The man on top swung his hips back and forward and back and forward into the girl. The two soldiers at the end of the bed bent her knees up and bowed them apart.

"*Rápido, Cerdo,*" said a soldier holding a foot and a knee. "*Hay diez más.*"

Blood wormed out of one of the girl's ears and stained the sheet. A swollen eyelid squinted on one side of her face. She stared at the ceiling as the man rammed into her on the screeching bed. She turned to the wall and clamped her teeth down on the gag, her chest heaving.

"*Mi capitán,*" said the man with Roger. "*Capturamos éste gringo con su barco en frente la isla.*"

The girl looked past the hunched-up soldier at Roger as the edge of her gag shook.

"*Díle al coronel,*" said the man holding a foot and a knee. "*Estamos ocupados. ¿No vés, maricón?*"

The humping soldier grunted and looked down, watching himself perform. He gripped the girl's breasts and bit one of her nipples as she squirmed. The captain tickled her foot and chuckled, slapping the panting soldier on the butt. The girl shut her eyes and uncurled her fists, and the men opened more space between her legs.

The bare-chested man shoved Roger outside and onto the porch. Lightning flashed again, lighting up a soldier with his pants unbuckled and the men sitting on the steps under the eaves, smoking. Roger slopped through the mud and the rain to the next bungalow, where up against a pole leaned Colonel Vargas, humming. Thunder rolled. The bare-chested man with the shotgun saluted.

"What's this?" said the colonel.

"I got lost," said Roger. "In the storm."

The colonel dipped his head sideways, and the soldier pushed Roger into the bungalow and turned on the light. Splashes of red smeared the bed sheet and the floor.

"Look," said Roger. "I don't know what you want . . ."

The guard hooked the back of Roger's neck and slammed his forehead against a wall, knocking him into a chair. Blood oozed from his temple into an eye.

"*Cabeza suave*," said the man. He strapped Roger's arms and legs to the chair. "*Pelota de caucho*."

"Zorro says your head is soft as a rubber ball," snickered the colonel, gold twinkling in his mouth.

"What do you want?" Blood dripped off the tip of Roger's nose onto the floor.

The colonel stood for a moment with his arms folded, gazing into the air.

"Can you give me Chicago?" He laughed and made a circling motion with his hand, and the bare-chested man wrenched a towel between Roger's teeth and tied it behind his neck.

Zorro swaggered out of the room with his shotgun pointed down, and Colonel Vargas followed, switching off the light and closing the door behind him, humming into the rain.

35

Floating in the sunlight that streamed through the window, flakes of dust swirled in slow-motion. Roger frowned; a scab twisted on his forehead. Blood and urine soaked his pants. He tipped his head sideways and swallowed.

Footsteps scuffled across the porch, and the door to the bungalow opened. The flashing blade of a machete appeared, then a leather cord snaked around a wrist, then an arm. Pepe crept into the room and closed the door as a volley of gunshots sounded down the beach. He went to the window and peered out a corner.

"Are you okay, señor?"

Roger grunted and nodded.

"They're killing the people," whispered Pepe. "For a casino. They want the island for a casino. They killed the *sargento* and Moonshot for this, so they can come and take everything. These soldiers killed Señor Ben and Mrs. Birdie, and I think Señor Smith. Some of the people they take in the boat and throw them in the water and watch. They just watch them, señor. The people who can't swim. They have their casinos in the city. Why they have to come here? Why they have to do this?"

A pair of boots sucked through the mud in front of the bungalow and climbed the steps. Roger shook his head and wiggled in the chair. Pepe crouched behind a dresser. The door opened. Cradling an automatic rifle in his arms, Colonel Vargas entered the room, humming.

"*Buenos días,*" grinned the colonel. He closed the door and walked toward Roger as the hum rattled in his throat.

The colonel's head twitched, and he turned toward the dresser. Roger pushed down, rocking the chair back and spearing the colonel's groin with his foot. The chair slammed into the floor, and the room filled with a flurry of hacking and metal banging on concrete.

A shadow swept across the ceiling. The bush knife dripped near Roger's face. His chest heaving, Pepe reached down and untied the gag from Roger's mouth. He pulled up the chair. In front of the door, blood streamed from the trunk of Colonel Vargas' body. Beside the dresser lay the colonel's severed head.

"Jesus Christ, Pepe."

The reports of gunshots echoed outside. Pepe slit the straps off Roger's feet and hands.

"The soldiers are in the other rooms and in the

restaurant. Some are on the beach."

Roger stood up and looked at the dead man's opened eyes. "Jesus Christ."

"They call him *El Pájaro de la Muerte,* The Bird of Death. He's the brother of the *generalísimo*."

"An army general?"

"The army, the navy, the post office, the bank . . . . Everything."

"Shit."

"He didn't even make a sound. Like a man with his fingers between the legs of a beautiful girl, who finds the beautiful girl is not a girl, but a man. Even without the head, the hand was still trying to shoot the gun." Pepe stared at the streaked machete, then picked up the rifle and handed it to Roger. "We'll go to the mountains. The people are hiding."

Roger followed him outside and off the porch to the jungle behind the bungalow. Drawing on vines and roots in the slush, slipping to his knees, he climbed, water spilling from the leaves and stinging the gash on his forehead. He rubbed his eyes and hugged his bandaged hand against his stomach. Gunshots rang from the hotel. Voices shouted. Roger and Pepe climbed higher and stopped in a clump of bushes and listened.

"They found him," said Pepe.

Roger swatted gnats from his face and squatted in the mud, squeezing his rifle, shaking. A green butterfly dashed from the foliage. Twigs snapped. Roger spun around with his rifle. Rain stood in the shadows gathering the air toward her with both hands.

"Come," she said. "This way."

Roger and Pepe scrambled behind her, and she led them up the mountain to her shack next to the monkeypod tree and brought Roger a clean shirt and pants and showed them to a refuge of branch shelters near a creek. People from the town cowered in the bushes. Roger stripped and mopped his body with cold water. The silk shirt sagged over his shoulders. He put on the pants and rolled the cuffs up off the ground.

In the mud under some trees, Pepe buried the old rags and sealed the hole with a log. They sat on rocks beside the creek and looked down at the town, patches of pink and blue buildings flickering between the branches in the breeze. Birds chirped. Gunshots rebounded up the mountainside. Through a clearing beside a bungalow, a soldier dragged a body, its heels trailing in the dirt. Silver sparkled on the water in the channel. Pepe dipped the machete into the creek and scrubbed the blade with his fingers.

"The people talk about these things on the mainland . . . in the small towns . . . in the mountains. But I never saw it before." He turned the knife over in the water. "*Sargento* de León was not like this."

"Why'd Moonshot stay with him?"

"The *guardia* always has a house and a job. He's a rich man without an election."

"She didn't love him?"

Pepe took the machete out of the creek and wiped it against his pants. "It's hard to love when you're hungry, no, señor?"

"Maybe we can get help."

Pepe shook his head. "We're the needle in the haystack."

"I can take a boat. There's guerrillas on the mainland."

"They're waiting for you to try this, señor."

"What else can we do?"

A man from the town crouched at the edge of the jungle, filing a knife against a stone.

"It makes no difference," said the man. "They take what they can. If they don't take it, somebody else will. And whoever takes it now will lose it later."

Gunfire sputtered in the distance. The man honed his knife. Shale clicked near the creek. The old woman hobbled forward with two plates of food and set them on a rock in front of Roger and Pepe. She lifted a strap off her shoulder and looped it up and over her head, loosening drawstrings and opening a bag.

"Take off the bandage," she said. "And wash the hand."

Roger unwrapped the wound and lowered his hand into the creek, hunching his shoulders and wincing as the water flushed the torn skin. From her pouch the old woman removed a strip of cloth and a packet of bundled paper. She unfolded the edges of the paper and tweezed a pinch of leaves between her fingers and soaked it in the stream. Grabbing Roger's elbow and crossing his arm on her lap, she padded the gum into his palm, molding it around the wound.

"The leaves are from the *Loa* tree?" asked Roger.

"No," said Rain.

In the bushes the knife blade rasped back and forth against the stone.

"I went there with Moonshot." He flinched. She pressed the cloth around his hand and bent down, splitting the end of the bandage with her teeth. "It smells like the one we burned."

She knotted the ends of the wrapping at the base of his wrist and repacked the rest of the leaves inside the paper. She put the packet in her bag and stood up. "You know what he said before he left?"

Roger looked at the old woman.

"He said he didn't know what was the right thing. He said he was going to do it anyway, and if I wanted to do it, too, I could. 'Don't be a fool,' I said. 'Life's hard for everyone.'"

The old woman smiled and stumbled across the rocks beside the creek toward her shack.

"Thank you," called Roger.

Pepe broke off a chunk of fish from his plate and tossed it into his mouth.

"What's she talking about?"

"I think the head's not right, señor." He tapped his skull with a finger. "It was a long time ago before I came to Isla Grande and before they had the hotel. They say her husband was killed by a tree."

The old woman disappeared through the bushes.

"A burning tree?"

Pepe shrugged and leaned over, scooping a handful of water from the creek and slurping. "All the world has a story, no, señor?"

The knife blade scraped against the stone. Roger gazed down the mountainside at the town, his shirt sleeves flapping on his arms in the breeze.

36

Early in the morning, through a tunnel of trees, Roger sidestepped down the mountain, hissing the earth over fallen leaves. He lowered his shoulder and stopped against a trunk, facing the slope, crouching low, resting his rifle across his knees. Out from the shadows glided an owl, banking into a beam of sunlight and vanishing.

An avalanche of dirt clods rushed through the bushes, and Pepe slid past on the seat of his pants, heels plowing up the sod, machete waving at hanging vines. A thump sounded below. Roger traced the furrow to a ledge behind the church and poked the muzzle of his rifle through a net of shrubs. Pepe lay sprawled on the ground in front of the church wall.

"You okay?"

He rolled over and stood up, brushing off his pants.

The crash of a shore breaker echoed off the mountain. Roger jumped down and walked to the end of the church and leaned around the corner.

"They're gone."

Pepe waddled to the edge of the building. "The *guardia?*"

"The boats."

Another wave cracked on the beach.

"Maybe they took them to the hotel."

Roger wiped the sweat off his face with a sleeve and nodded at the next building. "Quietly, okay?"

They dashed across the open space and jogged behind a row of houses. The stench of rotting flesh leaked out the shuttered windows; bullet holes gouged the walls; pieces of broken furniture lay scattered along the street. At the end of the line of houses, they entered the jungle under a canopy of dark leaves and specks of blue sky and followed the path toward the hotel, Roger's glance darting from side to side.

Turning into the hill at the first bungalow, they climbed above the beach and squatted in a shroud of ferns overlooking the restaurant and the wooden pier. Roger posted the gun butt on the ground and braced the weapon against his shoulder. The metal barrel chilled his ear. Out in the cove a white sheet of foam melted on the reef.

"You see anything, Pepe?"

"No, señor. Nothing. Maybe they're hiding in the rooms."

"Where's the boats?"

"Maybe they put them under the water."

"Sank them?"

"Maybe, señor."

Roger wound his way through the bushes down the hill and sprinted across a stretch of sand to the back of the hotel, creeping up the steps and nudging the door open with his gun barrel. He stepped inside. A woman's carcass lay butchered across a table. Slivered beer bottles and goblets covered the floor. He walked through the room and out the side past a dead man slumped at the door, clutching a hoe.

Down the stairs he trampled across the flower bed to the first bungalow and climbed the porch. Sparkling through the window, copper wires pinned a corpse to a red mattress. A second body sat slaughtered in the corner, its hands nailed to the wall. Roger backed off the stoop, shattering the glass with bullets and running across the sand to the water. Pepe caught him at the shore, and they walked down the beach to the sand spit that hooked out into the reef, and they stood, their shirt tails waving in the breeze.

"Even the monster can't kill the wind, no, señor?"

"We can make a raft," said Roger. "We can paddle across."

Pepe placed a hand on his chest. "One day, señor, when I was a small boy, my grandmother takes my hand and puts it on my chest like this. She says, 'Feel the heart, Pepe. You feel it?' I say, 'Yes, grandmother, I feel it.' My grandmother was *muy sabia,* very smart, and very old like the banyan tree.

"'When you are in the world, Pepe, use what you learn from all the things you see and from all the things you do. Use them for walking in the world.

"'Yes, grandmother,' I say. I think I already know how to walk, but I don't say this to her.

"'But when you are with the people, Pepe, remember to feel the heart. It is the same in all the people.'"

Pepe lowered his hand and looked at Roger. "It's not the same, señor."

"I don't know."

"But why some people feel this and some people don't?"

"I don't know, Pepe."

"Maybe they don't have a grandmother like mine, no, señor?"

The shriek of a whistle pierced the air, whizzing across the sky from the mainland. The mountaintop behind the hotel thundered. A tree burst into a cloud of smoke and flames. Roger dropped to his knees. A second whistle screamed into the restaurant, spinning slats of wood across the beach and checkering the roof with fire. Another explosion showered Roger and Pepe with saltwater and sand, and they ran toward the bungalows.

In front of a porch, a blast flattened them on the ground, spitting dirt over their heads and backs. The door to the building opened. Roger aimed his rifle. The dark boy from the mainland peered through the doorway.

"*Los soldados nos hicieron traerlos,*" said the boy.

Roger lowered the gun. "Where's your father?"

"*Papá.*" The boy looked behind him. "*Muerte.*"

"Dead," said Pepe.

The boy pointed into the room.

"Tell him to come with us."

"*Venga,*" said Pepe. "*Rápido.*"

The boy clasped the doorknob and stared into the room, and Pepe went up the steps and looked inside. He grabbed the boy by the arm and pulled him away, talking to him in Spanish. The three ran into the jungle, clawing up the slope in the shelling, Pepe's machete ahead, scything away stalks and vines.

A plane buzzed overhead, spiraling cylinders onto the island, incinerating the jungle in whooshes. Roger steadied the rifle against a tree and fired through the branches. The plane crossed behind the mountain. They climbed to the top of the hill and hid behind the iron door in the lighthouse. The buzzing faded away.

In the gusts of wind that eddied inside the tower, a purr arose and grew into the monotone of engines churning. Roger propped his rifle against the wall of the lighthouse and pounded up the metal staircase and outside onto the platform. Soot and ash prickled his eyes. He shielded his face with a hand.

"What is it, señor?" echoed Pepe's voice from below.

A cloud of black smoke billowed from the hotel. Trees flamed. In patches of orange and red, the island burned. Through the haze, out on the water, thin white lines threaded across the channel. Engines roared. The white streaks brightened.

"Boats," shouted Roger.

Across the length of the passage, the white scars rippled toward the island. Rifles gleamed in the sunlight, camouflaged fatigues stood out against the blue water. A gunboat docked at the main pier in town.

"Soldiers," yelled Roger.

"How many?"

"The whole goddamned army."

"The *generalísimo*."

Roger ran down the steps and took his rifle, and they went out onto the glade in front of the lighthouse.

"Where can we go?"

Pepe shook his head and pointed over the hill.

Down the back of the mountain, they coiled along a trail overhanging the surf. Pepe stopped and picked up the boy by the arms and dangled him over the ledge, dropping him onto another path. The two men lowered themselves down the wall by vines, and they shuffled sideways one by one with the dark boy between them, their backs to the island, their feet to the sea. The path ended at a niche cut into the moss and ferns where they huddled against each other. Waves banged below them on the rocks. A rainbow arched through the swirls of rising mist.

Pepe whispered to the boy. "You have to swim. Swim as far as you can. Let the water take you down the coast."

The boy stared at his feet.

"Swim, *mi hijo*." Pepe pointed to the ocean. "Swim. *¿No puedes nadar?*"

The boy shook his head.

"He can't swim," said Pepe.

Cast over the water, a column of shadows crossed the upper ledge and halted. A voice issued orders.

Dust sifted through the plants and trickled onto Roger's shoulder.

Pepe strapped the machete around his waist and grabbed the boy by the arms. "*No tengas miedo, mi hijo. Y no grites. Los soldados están arriba.* Swim." He hurled the boy off the cliff.

Arms swinging, the boy plunged feet first into the sea and floundered in the swells in front of the rocks. A covey of white birds shot away from the island. A shadow advanced down the lower ledge. Roger and Pepe crouched inside their hollow as a soldier's boots slid along the path. Both hands choking the handle, Pepe thrust his machete through the soldier's back, twisting the blade and dragging the man down to the ground. Blood dripped off the mint plants and the fat man's fingers.

"The boy," said Pepe. Footsteps pounded above. Voices called.

Roger stared at him.

"I can't swim," said Pepe. "You're the swimmer."

The dead man's blood dripped over the cliff. A gunshot rang in the air. Roger laid down his rifle on the ledge, and Pepe picked it up.

"Go," he said.

"I can't."

"Then we all die and no one knows what for. Go. Take the boy."

Roger stood up and kicked the dead soldier in the stomach, and the body lurched forward and fell off the cliff.

He dove, spray streaking across his face, the corpse

tumbling below him against the rocks. He hit the water and grabbed hold of the boy, swimming with him out to sea as boats filled with soldiers swarmed across the channel from the mainland and the fat man's red shorts faded into a dot on the emerald-green island.

ABOUT THE AUTHOR

Born in Los Angeles, California, Richard Hughes has traveled widely, barnstorming across the United States as a semi-professional baseball player, crossing the Bolivian Andes by jeep, and backpacking 5,000 miles through China. Mr. Hughes is a recipient of the Henri Coulette Award for Poetry from the Academy of American Poets. *Isla Grande* is his first novel.